Afterschool

The Dancing Kettle
The Magic Listening Cap
Takao and Grandfather's Sword
The Promised Year
Mik and the Prowler
New Friends for Susan
The Full Circle
Makoto, the Smallest Boy
Rokubei and the Thousand Rice Bowls
The Forever Christmas Tree
Sumi's Prize
Sumi's Special Happening
Sumi and the Goat and the Tokyo Express
The Sea of Gold
In-Between Miya
Hisako's Mysteries
Journey to Topaz
Samurai of Gold Hill
The Birthday Visitor
The Rooster Who Understood Japanese

Journey Home
A Jar of Dreams
(Margaret K. McElderry Books)

THE BEST
BAD THING

THE BEST
BAD THING

Yoshiko Uchida

A Margaret K. McElderry Book

Atheneum 1985 New York

Library of Congress Cataloging in Publication Data

Uchida, Yoshiko.
The best bad thing.
"A Margaret K. McElderry Book."
Summary: At first dismayed at having to spend
the last month of her summer vacation helping out
in the household of recently widowed Mrs. Hata,
Rinko discovers there are pleasant surprises for
her, but then bad things start to happen.
Sequel to "A Jar of Dreams."
[1. Japanese Americans—Fiction.   2. Family life—
Fiction.   3. Poverty—Fiction]   I. Title.
PZ7.U25Be   1983   [Fic]   83-2833
ISBN 0-689-50290-7

Published simultaneously in Canada by
McClelland & Stewart, Ltd.
Composed by Maryland Linotype Composition Company, Inc.
Baltimore, Maryland
Manufactured by Fairfield Graphics
Fairfield, Pennsylvania
First Printing August 1983
Second Printing May 1984
Third Printing January 1985
Fourth Printing June 1985

*For Chie and George
and their grandson, Andrew*

THE BEST
BAD THING

1

"MAMA, DO I ABSOLUTELY HAVE TO GO?"
I asked for the third time.

The last thing I wanted to do was go out to East
Oakland to visit Mrs. Hata after church. Everybody said
she was a little crazy. And I believed them, even though
she and Mama come from the same town in Japan and are
good friends. My best friend, Tami, says Mrs. Hata has
bats in the belfry.

I tried once more. "Do I, Mama?"

But Mama didn't pay any attention to me. She was
busy making rice balls for the picnic lunch she was taking to Mrs. Hata's. She'd spoon up a paddle full of
steaming rice, wet and dip her fingers in salt, and then
shape the rice into an egg-shaped oval. The hot rice was
turning her palms red, but I guess Mama's hands are so
used to being stuck in hot water in our home laundry,
they don't feel much of anything anymore.

Mama just kept right on making rice balls and lining

1

them up in neat rows in a black lacquer box. She put a red pickled plum in the middle of some so they'd resemble the Japanese flag, with its red ball of sun on a field of white.

Papa loves those pickled plums, but I sure don't. They are so sour, they cover me with goose bumps and make my tongue curl.

"Here, Rinko," Mama said, pushing the lacquer box toward me, "put the sesame seeds on these for me."

I started sprinkling the white rice balls with the tiny black seeds so they looked as though the ants had already got to them. But all the time I was trying to figure out how to get out of going to Mrs. Hata's. Mama didn't seem to realize I had some plans of my own.

Suddenly she answered me, as though she'd just heard what I'd asked five minutes ago.

"Of course we have to go," she said. "It's the forty-ninth-day anniversary of Mr. Hata's death."

The way Mama said it, I knew it was an important Japanese custom and there wasn't much point in arguing. But I did anyway.

"Tami and I were going to see *Tarzan of the Apes* at the Lorin this afternoon," I explained, as though it was vitally necessary for us to go.

I didn't tell her I was planning to use the ten cents she had given me that week for helping her with the laundry. Actually, I'm supposed to put any money I earn in my "going to college jar," but I thought Mama wouldn't mind if I gave myself a treat once in a while.

2

Going to see a movie on a Sunday, however, isn't exactly Mama's idea of a treat. To her it's more like committing a major sin. For a long time, Mama had all of us believing that Sundays were meant only for going to church and being solemn. And it was only after my big brother Cal went to college that he developed some ideas of his own about Sundays. One day he and Mama had a huge fight about it, and Papa sided with Cal.

"Times are changing, Mama," Papa told her. "This is 1935 and there are worse sins than going to a movie on a Sunday."

So Mama finally gave in. That was over a year ago, and ever since, Cal's done pretty much what he wants on Sundays, or any other day for that matter. That means that Joji (my younger brother, ten and a half and a real pest) and I can do more on Sundays too—except when there's something really important to Mama like this anniversary of Mr. Hata's death.

Cal was lucky. He was up in Alaska working in a salmon cannery for the summer and probably sinning like crazy every Sunday.

It wasn't only that I wanted to go to the movies. I really didn't want to make an anniversary-of-a-death call. After all, it wasn't as though you were celebrating something pleasant like a birthday or a wedding anniversary. I wasn't sure how I was supposed to act. Sorry and sad, as if you were at a funeral? Or happy that Mr. Hata had been in Heaven for forty-nine days? Or maybe

3

it was like the Obon Festival, when the spirits of the deceased are supposed to come home for a visit and everybody makes a lot of food to celebrate.

Mama can be pretty stubborn when she wants to, but so can I. I wasn't going to give up without a really good try.

"*Tarzan of the Apes* will be gone by next Sunday," I said glumly.

Mama didn't answer, and if Joji hadn't walked in then and opened his big mouth, Mama might have come around. But old Joji spoiled everything.

"It sure is gonna be fun seeing Zenny and Abu," he said.

And before Mama could stop him, he picked up one of her rice balls and popped the whole thing in his mouth. Joji loves to eat and stuffs himself at every opportunity. I could have wrung his neck for looking so happy about going to the Hatas'. I could tell Mama was about to say, "Look at Joji. He doesn't mind going to visit Mrs. Hata. He's not complaining."

Actually Joji had no reason to complain because he would have a good time with Mrs. Hata's two boys, Zenny and Abu. They'd go walk on the railroad tracks or maybe even hitch a ride if there were any freight cars coming down the feeder line.

Zenny was about the same age as my brother, but Abu was two years younger, and Joji loved having somebody he could boss around for a change.

I gave my brother a dirty look. "Mama and I were

4

2

AS THINGS TURNED OUT THAT SUNDAY,
we didn't get home until almost suppertime because
right after we ate Mama's lunch in Mrs. Hata's kitchen,
we all went out in the fields to help pick cucumbers.

Actually it wasn't as easy as I thought it would be.
The cucumbers weren't staked. They were just sprawling
on the ground, so we had to crawl on our hands and knees
to find the ones ready for picking. I put the ones I picked
in a basket, and when my basket was full, I emptied it
on the sorting table.

It wasn't really a table. It was a stand that Mr. Hata
had built with dividers, so the cucumbers could be
separated by size into ones, twos, threes, and "the
crooks"—the crooked ones.

We all spread out in the fields, and I could see Joji
and Zenny and Abu horsing around, using the cucumbers
for guns and bang-banging at each other.

"Hey," I yelled at them. "Get to work."

11

But they didn't pay the slightest attention to me. I could have been talking to a basketful of cucumbers.

Papa piled a dozen burlap sacks full of cucumbers on the back of Mrs. Hata's truck so she could take them to the factory first thing in the morning.

She kept thanking Papa, saying, "Mr. Hata and I are so grateful," as though her husband was still alive.

Tami was right, I thought to myself. She *is* crazy.

By the time we got home, Mama was too tired to cook, so we just had some cold leftover rice with canned tuna. I was still hungry when we finished eating, but what Mama said made me forget everything, even my half-empty stomach.

Whenever Mama has something important to say, she usually says it when we're all sitting down together for supper. Sometimes she'll blurt it out right after she says grace, which is a shorter version of the long rambling conversation she has with God every night. But other times she'll wait until Papa has had the bowl of rice with hot tea and pickles that he has at the end of every meal. Like the time she announced she wanted to start a home laundry to help Papa pay his bills. I was flabbergasted when Mama came up with that idea. And now she flabbergasted me again.

"I've been thinking . . ." she said, and she pushed some stray hair into the bun at the back of her neck the way she does when she's not quite sure how to say what she wants to say.

Here it comes, I thought. Now Mama's going to say

she wants to go help Mrs. Hata for a while. And I was all ready to say I'd take care of everything at home while she was gone. But I couldn't have been more mistaken.

She wanted to help Mrs. Hata, all right. But *she* wasn't the one who would be going to East Oakland. It was *me* she wanted to ship off for the rest of the summer.

"You still have another month of summer vacation, Rinko," Mama said. "And you saw how much help Mrs. Hata needs, not just in the fields, but with the housework too."

I saw all right, but I certainly didn't want to volunteer to go help her.

"Just having you there would be a comfort to her," Mama added. And she gave my hand a pat as though to make sure I knew what a great comfort I was to her too.

"I thought *you'd* be the one to go," I said lamely.

But Mama said she couldn't possibly leave us to fend for ourselves and run the laundry too.

"I could manage," I offered. "I know I could."

But Mama said that was out of the question. "There's a lot more to running the house and the laundry than you think, Rinko."

"But who'll empty the water pan under the icebox if I go? Who'll feed the chickens and collect the eggs and iron the pillowcases and clean the house on Saturdays?" I asked, ticking off my chores one by one.

When Mama said Joji could do all that, I saw I needed to be more direct. "Well, I don't want to go," I said.

"Not even for one month?"

13

"No, Mama. I *really* don't want to."

I certainly didn't want to go live in that spooky old house with those two pesky boys. That would be like having two Jojis in my hair all day.

"Besides, everybody says Mrs. Hata is a little crazy," I said, trying a new tack. "They say she got that way after she lost her second baby girl."

I knew her first little girl died of diphtheria when she was two, and the other one died of scarlet fever when she was only a tiny baby. I guess that would be enough to make anybody a little crazy.

Until then Papa had just been sitting there, leaning back in his chair, stroking his mustache and listening to Mama and me carry on. But the minute he heard what I said about Mrs. Hata, he got into the discussion.

"Rinko," he said, "there is nothing wrong with Mrs. Hata. She may be a little eccentric, but she is *not* crazy."

And the way he said it, I knew he was disappointed in me for repeating idle gossip.

"They don't even have a phone," I said, beginning to feel desperate. "How can I call home or Tami?" I'd forgotten I was mad at her.

"I'll go, then," Joji suddenly piped up. And for once I thought he'd had a bright idea.

"Swell," I said. "Let Joji go."

I started to leave the table to show I considered the discussion ended, but Papa wasn't finished with me yet.

"She needs someone she can depend on, Rinko," he said.

And Mama immediately agreed with him. The two of

them are usually on the same side of an argument except when Mama goes on about what's sinful and what's not. Then Papa usually sides with Joji or me.

I honestly think Papa goes to church mainly to please Mama. He says God is just as much out in the park or the open fields as He is inside our dark, musty Japanese church. That's what I think, too.

"You're older and more responsible, Rinko," Mama said, knowing how to get to me. "And what Mrs. Hata needs now is someone like a daughter she can talk to. She's lonely, Rinko, and needs company and comfort as much as help."

What could I say when Mama and Papa said things like that? They made me feel it was my Christian duty to go. And I certainly didn't want to get in trouble with God, who was Mama's Personal Friend.

I guess Joji knew he didn't have a chance now. He wiped his mouth with the back of his hand and got up from the table.

"OK, Rink, *you* go then," he said, and he went banging off to his room.

"Well . . . can I come home in two weeks if I don't like it out there?" I asked, beginning to cave in.

"Of course," Mama reassured me. "I have Ladies Aid Meeting next Sunday, but we'll be out the Sunday after that to see how you're getting along."

"When do I have to go?"

Papa said he'd drive me out on Wednesday morning, since that was usually a quiet day for his repair shop.

"I'll bet Mrs. Hata will be surprised to see me," I said.

15

But Mama only smiled. And I knew then she'd probably already told Mrs. Hata I'd be out to help her.

I'd never been away from home before, except for the times I'd slept over at Tami's house, but they didn't really count because that's like being at home. Except, of course, Tami's mother with her bulging overactive-thyroid eyes really makes me nervous. She has to know everything about everybody, and she's always trying to squeeze some news from me about the people at church. Someday I think I'll tell her the minister ran off with the deacon's wife. That would really make her eyes bulge.

I went through all the clothes in my closet and checked my drawers, trying to decide what to take. Not that I have so many possessions, but I felt as though I needed to take some familiar things so I wouldn't feel too lonely.

I didn't want to admit it to anybody, but actually I was sort of scared about going to Mrs. Hata's . . . well, not scared exactly, but uncomfortable. I really didn't know her all that well because whenever we went to see her, I tried to avoid her as much as possible. I guess it was because of what people said about her. And now, here I was about to go live with her for two weeks. It gave me the creeps.

I decided to take a few Seaman mysteries to read, since I'd be miles from a library, and if I was going to live in a spooky house, I might as well read something scary and mysterious.

16

I also packed my five-year diary with the red leather cover and the tiny gold lock and key that Cal gave me last Christmas. Every night I write in it all the things that have happened to me that day. But whoever made the diary certainly wasn't very bright, because there are only five lines for each day. And who can possibly squeeze a whole day into a one-inch space? What I do is spill over into the space for next year, and sometimes even into 1938 and 1939.

Whenever I write in my diary, I usually lock the three doors of my room and hang my "Do Not Disturb" signs on them so no one will barge in from the hall or Mama and Papa's room or the back room where Joji and Cal sleep. It's a trial and tribulation to live in a room right smack in the middle of the house, with everyone tramping through it to get to the phone or the bathroom. I just hoped I'd have a private room at Mrs. Hata's.

Papa brought one of Mama's old suitcases up from the basement for me. It was a brown leather one with straps, which Mama had brought when she came from Japan to marry Papa.

I looked at all the stuff I'd laid out on my bed and told Papa I might need another suitcase.

"You're only staying for one month, you know," Papa said, smiling.

But I guess he saw the forlorn look on my face and understood why I needed to take more than just my clothes and clean underwear. And he went back to the basement to look for another suitcase for me. Papa is very quick to understand how I feel, even if I can't find the words to tell him. He knows how to read my face, just the way Mama seems to be able to see inside my skull and know exactly what I am thinking.

I felt as though I were going a thousand miles from home. I decided to forgive Tami, and I called to tell her to write me every day.

"You mean the mailman actually goes way out there?" she asked, making me feel worse than I already did.

"Of course," I answered, even though I didn't remember seeing a mailbox anywhere.

"Well, good luck," Tami said, as though I'd be needing it.

When I'd finished packing, I went next door to say good-bye to our neighbor, Mrs. Sugarman. Mrs. Sugar— which is what I call her—is also one of my best friends, even though she's a white lady and about fifty years older than I am. The funny thing is, I can tell her just about everything, even things I can't tell Mama or Papa or my big brother, Cal.

I told her once how miserable I felt when the white kids at school treated me as though I didn't exist. And she said, "Never you mind, Rinko. They're just stupid and don't know any better. You know something? I feel sorry for *them* for being so stupid. That's what!" And she gave me some hot cocoa and sugar cookies to make me feel better.

"Isn't it awful?" I said, telling her about going to help Mrs. Hata. "It's the worst thing that's happened to me all summer!"

18

Mrs. Sugar didn't say how nice it was that I was going to do my Christian duty. She just said, "Why, I'm going to miss you, Rinko." And she gave me a bag of cookies to take in case there weren't any at Mrs. Hata's.

Early Wednesday morning Papa put my two suitcases in the back seat of his car, and I was ready to leave for East Oakland. I felt the way I did the day Cal went off to Alaska. I absolutely hate good-byes, even temporary ones, and I had to blink hard to keep from crying when Cal left.

"What're you crying for, Rink?" Cal asked. "I'll be back by September."

"I know," I said. But I didn't really. What if his ship hit an iceberg and sank? What if his foot got caught in the machinery at the cannery and he got mangled? What if he liked Alaska so much he didn't want to come home? I was doing it again. I was "what iffing." I gave Cal a hug, which I know he didn't like, and said, "You'd better come back or I'm really going to be mad at you."

I was mad at Mama now for shipping me off to East Oakland and for causing me to be separated from her and Papa and Joji and Mrs. Sugar. What if something happened to me and I never came back?

Mama gave me a hug and a basket of fresh eggs to take to Mrs. Hata. Joji gave me a poke and said, "Lucky bum, you'll get to ride the freights."

But lucky was the last thing I was feeling. What I felt was homesick, even before I left.

Papa cranked up the motor, I climbed in the front

19

seat, and we started off. It wasn't often I got to ride up in front with Papa because that's where Cal or Joji usually sat. In fact, it wasn't often that Papa and I went anyplace, just the two of us.

He drove real fast since Mama wasn't in the back seat telling him to slow down. He was humming and acting as though we were on our way to a picnic. But the fog was coming in from San Francisco bay, the way it does in the summer, and I felt as though it were creeping into my stomach and settling there, all cold and clammy.

Papa glanced sideways at me and said, "You'll enjoy yourself, Rinko. I think you'll like Mrs. Hata."

I noticed he didn't mention the two boys.

"You know," he added, "I think Mrs. Hata is the only Japanese woman I know who can drive a truck."

I knew he was right. None of Mama's Japanese women friends would have dreamed of learning how to drive. In fact, not many Japanese families even owned cars, and when they did, it was always the father who drove. We wouldn't have had a car either if somebody hadn't sold Papa the old Model T for $30 and he'd fixed the engine himself.

"Is she any good at driving that old truck you fixed up for Mr. Hata?"

Papa nodded. "That lady's got a lot of gumption. You'll see."

Maybe, just maybe, I thought, I could like a lady who drove a truck. And pretty soon I was singing, "O beautiful for spacious skies, For amber waves of grain. . . ."

Papa stuck out his chin, cleared his throat, and chimed in.

"For purple mountain majesties, Above the fruited plain! . . ."

We were both bellowing like a couple of moose when we got there—not to any fruited plains, but to Mrs. Hata's shabby old house. I took one look at it, and my spirits began to sink again.

3

Mrs. Hata was out in front with Zenny and Abu when we drove up. They'd just finished loading more cucumbers on their truck and were on their way to the factory.

"You're just in time to go with us, Rinko," Mrs. Hata called out to me. She cranked up the motor of her truck and told me to get in front with her.

"What'll I do with my suitcases?" I asked. "And here, Mama sent you some fresh eggs."

"Oh, just leave everything on the front porch," she answered. "They'll be safe."

But I certainly wasn't about to leave my worldly possessions and a basketful of fresh eggs on their porch for some hobo to walk off with. I gave Papa a desperate look, and right away he saw my problem. He heaved my suitcases onto the back of the truck where Zenny and Abu were already perched on the sacks of cucumbers.

"Here, you boys take care of these suitcases for Rinko,

will you?" he asked, and he gave me the eggs to carry up in front.

"Sure, OK," Zenny said.

"Sure, OK," Abu echoed and immediately sat on my big brown suitcase.

"Hey, be careful," I yelled at him.

He was on the chubby side, with a round face and hair combed down over his forehead. He looked a lot like Joji, except he wore little round glasses because he was nearsighted. I guessed he liked to eat every bit as much as Joji, because he certainly made a big dent in my suitcase when he plopped down on top of it.

Both the boys were wearing the same faded shirts, overalls, and scruffy shoes they had on when I last saw them. But today they both wore wool caps. Zenny's was pulled down over his forehead, but Abu had flipped his visor back.

Mrs. Hata had the motor roaring and looked as though she was about to take off, so I said good-bye to Papa and climbed in front with her.

"We'll take good care of Rinko, Mr. Tsujimura," she called out to Papa. "Thank you for lending me your daughter for a while."

Papa waved his cap. "I hope she'll be helpful."

Then Mrs. Hata charged off down the dirt road, and I knew immediately she liked to drive just like Papa—fast. I felt like Mama, wanting to yell, "Not so fast! Not so fast!" But instead I said, "You sure are a good driver, Mrs. Hata."

23

She answered me in Japanese. She said she understood English pretty well but didn't feel comfortable speaking it. "It makes me feel odd—like when I've put my undershirt on backwards. You know?"

I knew exactly what she meant. "Like when I have to talk in Japanese."

"Well, anyway, just call me Auntie," she said. "After all, you're going to be my daughter for a while."

"Just a month," I reminded her, although I was thinking maybe only two weeks to myself. I wanted to be sure she knew there was a limit to my Christian charity.

She nodded, as though she didn't want to think about when I'd be leaving.

"You've got very nice earlobes," she said suddenly. "They'll hold a grain of rice, and that means you'll have good fortune all your life."

"Really? That's swell."

I felt my earlobes while I stole a sideways look at Auntie Hata. She was wearing an old cotton dress that looked as if it had been washed a hundred times. It wasn't ironed very well, and I was thinking I could do a lot better and not leave so many wrinkles.

Her straight black hair was pulled into a big bun in back, just like Mama's and all the other Japanese ladies' I know. Her face was full and round, like Abu's, with smooth, ruddy skin. In fact, her cheeks looked like ripe plums ready to burst. Unlike Mama, who is small and skinny, Mrs. Hata was big and plump.

The truck swerved for a minute as Auntie Hata turned

24

to look at me. Then she told me how Mr. Hata had taught her to drive. "I had to learn because Mr. Hata was sick so much, you know. And then he went off to Los Angeles."

Papa had told me why he left. It was because Mr. Hata had tuberculosis and Papa thought the warmer weather down there might cure him. In fact, the last time I saw Mr. Hata he was coughing all the time and looked as pale as a green grape.

Papa wanted him either to go to Highland Hospital or to Los Angeles. But Mr. Hata said nobody ever came out of the hospital alive and that he'd never go there.

Well, I guess he got so bad, Mama and Papa worried that Zenny and Abu would catch TB too. So they finally talked Mr. Hata into going down to Los Angeles to stay with a friend. But he never did get better. And when he finally came home, it was in a wooden coffin.

Mama and Papa felt terrible about it. And I guess that's why they wanted me to come help Mrs. Hata. I think they felt a little responsible about Mr. Hata, although Papa says he would have died even sooner if he'd stayed up here.

I knew Auntie Hata was remembering Mr. Hata and wishing he was still here. "I bet Mr. Hata'd be proud of you if he could see you driving now," I said. I thought that would make her feel better.

"I guess he would, at that," she said. And then, "You know, I eat a clove of garlic every day. That's how I keep healthy."

I was almost as surprised as when she'd handed me

25

the cucumber. Here I thought we were discussing Mr. Hata, and suddenly she was talking about garlic. "Huh?" I said.

But Auntie Hata was finished talking about garlic too because we'd come to the factory, and she pulled up beside the loading dock. Before I could tell her I hate garlic, she sort of groaned as though her back still ached and eased herself out of the truck.

I tried to help unload the cucumbers, but I guess I got in the way more than anything else. Zenny talked to the foreman and made sure his mother got all the money coming to her. He counted it twice and then gave it to his mother, who put it in a small coin purse in her pocket. I guess now that his papa was gone, Zenny had to be the man of the family. He certainly seemed a lot older than my brother, Joji, even though they were about the same age.

Auntie Hata told me to ride home with the boys in back now that there was more room, and I was glad to be where I could keep an eye on my suitcases. Zenny pushed them back close to the cab so they wouldn't fall off.

He was as tall as I was but not as scrawny, and I noticed he had large eyes like his mother's, with long, dark lashes. What a waste, I thought. I would have given anything to have his eyes and lashes instead of my small eyes with their stumpy lashes. Life is very unfair. But at least I had better earlobes. Zenny's didn't look as though they'd hold a thing, let alone a grain of rice.

"Why'd you bring two suitcases for, anyway?" he asked me.

And immediately Abu added, "What's inside them, anyways?"

I leaned up against the suitcases so Abu wouldn't sit on them. "Clothes and stuff."

"What kind of stuff?" Abu edged closer.

I could tell he was dying to get into my belongings and the last thing I needed was a little eight year old rummaging through my possessions.

"They're my private and personal belongings," I said.

"Huh?"

"She means keep hands off," Zenny explained.

"You're pretty smart, Zenichiro Hata," I said.

But the minute I said that, I wished I hadn't, because now Zenny had to show me exactly how smart he was. He pointed to a hole about the size of a tin can in the floor of the truck.

"Carved that myself with a pocketknife," he said proudly.

"Oh?" I didn't think that was anything to be so excited about.

"Y'know what it's for, don'tcha?" Abu asked.

I knew by the grin on his little round face that it was something I wouldn't want to know about.

"No, I don't, and I don't care," I said, trying to sound lofty and cold. He told me anyway.

"It's to pee in when we can't wait," he said. "Here, I'll show ya." And Abu began to unbutton his fly.

Zenny and Abu were both watching my face to see how I'd react. I knew the way I behaved in the next minute could either make my life miserable or bearable for the

27

next two weeks. I felt my face getting red and knew even my earlobes were burning up. But I just stared hard at Abu, ready to stare him down. Any time my brother Joji and I have a stare-down, I usually win because I can keep from blinking, even if my eyes begin to water.

Abu was almost at the last button, so I said calmly and coolly in a school-teacher-like voice, "Go right ahead, Abu. You just pee in your hole if you want to."

That really surprised him, and he turned to look at his big brother, not quite knowing what to do. Zenny looked at Abu and then he looked at me and finally he said, "Cut it out, Abu. That ain't nice."

Abu looked disappointed, but he buttoned up his pants, and I knew I'd probably passed the test they'd planned for me. But just to make sure Abu understood he couldn't mess around with me, I glared at him and used his full given name. "You'd just better watch yourself, Abraham."

Mr. Hata had named Abu after Abraham Lincoln, whom he admired greatly, but Mrs. Hata couldn't pronounce his name. She used to call him Abu-ra-hamu, but that got to be too much trouble, and she just called him Abu. So did everybody else.

I knew Abu hated his name, and Zenny didn't like his either. He was called Zenichiro after his grandpa in Japan. But none of his teachers could say it, so they just called him Zenny.

I always think it's too bad we can't choose our own names and are stuck with the ones our parents give us

28

when we're too small and dumb to know any better. I really feel sorry for my big brother, Cal, whose real name is California. Imagine being stuck with that all your life! Any time I want to get his goat, I just call him California, and it's like waving a red flag in front of a bull.

I'm not so crazy about Rinko either, because the kids call me Rinky-dink. If I could have chosen my own name, I would have picked something poetic like Ophelia or Evangeline. But I guess I'm lucky not to be stuck with something like Sweet Pea or Honeysuckle, since Mama is crazy about flowers and said she almost named me after one. A friend of mine was almost called Lavoris because her mama thought it sounded pretty until she found out it was a mouthwash.

Abu reacted the way my brother does when I call him by his honest and true name—like an angry bull.

"Don't call me that!" he yelled, doubling up his fist.

"OK, I won't if you keep hands off everything in my suitcases. In fact, everything in my room. OK?"

Abu stuck out his grimy hand. "OK. Shake," he said.

"Shake," I answered and suddenly felt a damp, clammy turtle wriggling in my hand.

I screamed and threw the turtle back at Abu.

"All right for you, Abraham Hata! That was a mean trick," I yelled. I'm not really sure what I mean when I say, "all right for you," but it's my all-purpose threat, which usually works on Joji.

Zenny was laughing so hard, he had to hold his

stomach, but finally he said, "Aw, Herbert ain't gonna hurt ya. He's just Abu's pet."

Before I could answer him, Zenny pointed toward the open fields and said, "I think I see something."

"What?" I asked, glad to change the subject.

Zenny and Abu looked at each other. Then Zenny leaned closer to me. "It's the spirits," he whispered. "It's my pa and baby sisters coming back from the land of the spirits to see us."

"Aw, you're making that up," I said.

"No, I'm not."

"Then tell me what they look like."

"Sorta like flickering lights."

"How do you know they're spirits? Maybe they're fireflies."

Zenny and Abu shook their heads. "No, they're not. You'll see," they said solemnly.

The fog was blowing in again and settling over the fields. And I felt a sudden chill. The dried weeds didn't look like amber waves now, they were more the color of ashes and dust.

"I don't believe you for one minute," I said to Zenny and Abu. But deep inside, I did just a little.

4

·•·

AS SOON AS WE GOT HOME FROM THE factory Auntie Hata took me upstairs to show me my room. I thought the house was really strange. Everything, including the stairs to the second floor, seemed to be sagging. It was as though a bunch of tired carpenters had put the house together and hadn't hammered the nails in hard enough. The house creaked and groaned when we walked around, as if it was trying to tell us to tread gently. I sincerely hoped no big wind would blow and cause it to collapse while I was in it.

There were no rugs on the floor, no electric lights (only kerosene lamps,) no telephone, no radio, and no icebox (only a screened cooler).

Another strange thing, there wasn't a single clock in the entire house. The first time I visited the Hatas I asked Zenny how they ever knew what time it was, and he told me they could tell by the trains.

The Western Pacific Railroad ran a few miles from

their house, and there was a feeder line only ten yards from their front gate, where freight trains ran to the lumberyard at East Fourteenth.

"We know it's time to leave for school when the first train goes by in the morning," Zenny had said.

"But how do you know when to eat lunch and supper?"

Zenny shrugged. "We eat when Ma tells us to."

I guessed that could be almost any time, since Auntie Hata seemed to do things whenever the mood struck her. Papa would go crazy here, I thought. He likes to have supper at six-thirty sharp, and that is exactly when Mama rings her black bell to call us all in to supper.

Now Auntie Hata opened the door to my room and said, "It's not fancy, but at least the roof doesn't leak."

She certainly was right about it's not being fancy. There was one window with no curtains, only a torn green shade rolled halfway down. And all there was in the small room was a narrow cot and an old bureau that looked as though it had been painted a dozen times. It was blue now, but I could see red where the blue had chipped off and some yellow beneath the red.

"We got that from the Salvation Army," Auntie Hata said about the bureau.

She sat on the cot then and gave it a little bounce to make sure it wouldn't collapse and told me that Mama had gotten the cot for her a long time ago from the dormitory at our church.

Mrs. Hata doesn't come to our church, although I know Mama's tried to get her to. I think the only time she did was for Mr. Hata's funeral. Mama and Papa made all the arrangements for her, and I happen to know they had to talk her out of keeping Mr. Hata's ashes in a small urn in her living room.

Actually, she wanted to keep his ashes until she saved up enough money to take them back to his village cemetery in Japan. But that might have taken twenty years. Mama and Papa explained that it wasn't proper—maybe it was even against the law—to keep his ashes in her house. So she finally let them bury his remains in the Mountain View Cemetery.

She kept a photo of Mr. Hata on the living room mantel instead, and the day I arrived there was a tiny dish of rice and a marigold in a bud vase beside it. She didn't have a home shrine because she isn't Buddhist. But then she isn't a Christian either. I don't exactly know what she is, except that she's Japanese.

Thank goodness Mr. Hata's ashes weren't on the mantel, I thought. If I were a spirit and got stuck in a small urn on the living room mantel, I would certainly want to come out and roam around a little at night.

I was wondering if Auntie Hata had ever seen Mr. Hata's spirit floating around the house. I guess I was staring at her in an odd way because she suddenly said, "I'll make a bath for you tonight, Rinko," as though she were offering to make me a chocolate cake or something I would enjoy.

"Where?" I asked. I still hadn't seen a bathtub in the house.

33

"Wherever you like. In the kitchen or outside."

I told her I'd never taken a bath outside before.

"Oh, it's lovely, Rinko. You soak in a tub with the hot water right up to your neck, and instead of a ceiling there's the whole sky filled with stars."

It sounded wonderful. I told her I definitely wanted an outside bath. So after we'd finished supper and the dishes, Zenny helped her carry out a square tin tub from the basement. They set it up at the side of the house on a grate over a shallow hole lined with bricks, and Auntie Hata built a small fire under the tub while Zenny filled it with the hose.

I was afraid I'd get boiled alive like a lobster inside that thing, but Auntie Hata banked the fire and put a wood float into the tub so I wouldn't get scorched. Then she set out a wooden platform beside it and Zenny strung up some rope and hung some old sheets around three sides of the tub. The fourth side was open so I could look out at the fields.

"There," Auntie Hata said when everything was ready. "You take first bath since you are our guest."

And she showed me how to wash and rinse myself on the little platform before I got into the tub to soak. That way the water would stay clean for the others.

"Just like in Japan," she said proudly.

I washed myself as fast as I could and climbed into the deep tub. The wood float sank beneath me and the water gurgled while I let myself down lower and lower until the water came right up to my chin.

34

I looked up and it was just like Auntie Hata said. There must've been a million stars spread out across the sky, as though somebody had scattered a handful of diamonds in a huge black bowl.

I wished they really were diamonds and I could have just one tiny one to give to Mama. All she has is a thin, gold wedding band. I never thought about her wanting jewelry or even wanting to dress up in a lot of fine clothes, I only thought about Mama the way I see her every day, wearing an apron and doing the washing and cooking. Her hair is never marcelled with waves and she never puts makeup on her face. But one day she told me she wished she could have a small diamond ring. I was surprised.

"It's just that I'd like something to leave for you, Rinko," she said. "Something that will last . . . something to remember me by."

It gave me the shivers to hear her say that. "You're never going to die, Mama," I told her. But deep inside, in a place I didn't want to look at or listen to, I knew some day she would. Just like Mr. Hata.

Naturally Mama, who can see inside my skull, knew immediately what I was thinking. She suddenly brushed herself all over, as though she were brushing away dust and lint.

"There," she said. "I've brushed away all the bad thoughts." And she never talked again about wanting a diamond ring. At least not to me.

It was really peaceful sitting there in the tub. I could

35

smell the eucalyptus branches smoldering beneath me, and I heard the crickets out in the fields. All the time I was soaking I kept an eye on the fields, watching for flickering lights. But I didn't see a thing.

Suddenly I heard footsteps crunching down the path from the road. What if it was a burglar, I thought, or a hobo who'd seen our lights?

I scrunched down in the tub, since there was no place else to go. And when the footsteps got closer, I took a deep breath, held my nose, and ducked under the water. I stayed there until I thought my lungs would burst, and when I came up, I heard the barn door slam.

I jumped out of the tub, put on my pajamas without even drying myself, and burst into the kitchen.

"Auntie Hata! Auntie Hata! There's somebody in the barn!"

Auntie Hata was sitting in one of the kitchen chairs, and Abu was standing behind her pounding the knots out of her shoulder muscles with his fists.

"Harder, Abu," Auntie Hata was telling him. "Pound harder."

Zenny was hunched over the kitchen table gluing a diamond kite together. Not one of them seemed the least bit interested in what I was saying.

"There's somebody in the barn!" I yelled again. "Maybe it's a burglar."

Auntie Hata finally stood up, leaving Abu with his fists still clenched. "Why, that must be Mr. Yamanaka," she said, as calm as a Buddha.

"Who?"

"The old man," Zenny explained, without even look-ing up.

"What old man?"

"The one who lives in the barn," Abu said, as though he were explaining something to a three year old.

"Well, nobody told me," I said, beginning to feel stupid standing there with my damp pajamas stuck to me and water still dripping from my hair.

Auntie Hata grabbed a dish towel and patted the water off my face and head. Mama would've had a fit if she'd seen her do that. Mama is so fussy she even separates "clean wash" from "dirty wash" when she does the laundry.

Dish towels are "clean wash" because they're used for drying the dishes, and they're washed first while the water's clean. "You wouldn't want to eat off a dish wiped with a cloth that was washed with dirty socks, would you?" Mama asks. And I guess I wouldn't.

Well, Auntie Hata just kept drying me off with her dish towel and telling me about the old man.

"He's lived in our barn for about a year, but he keeps pretty much to himself. He's a cook at The Eagle Cafe on Seventh Street, and walks to and from work every day."

For a minute I forgot about my soggy self. "All the way from Seventh Street? That must be almost a hundred blocks."

"If he was smart, he'd hitch a ride," Zenny remarked. He'd just finished tying some strips of cloth to his kite's tail and was holding it up to see how it looked.

37

"And that's another thing," Auntie Hata said, as though she was continuing a conversation I'd interrupted with all my screaming and hollering. "I don't want you boys riding those freight cars anymore. A little boy got killed last week doing that, and I don't want you to do it ever again. You hear, Zenny?"

"I hear."

"You keep Abu away from those freights too. Understand?"

"OK, Ma," Zenny said without looking up. But I saw he had his fingers crossed.

"Now you get into some dry pajamas and go to bed," she said to me as if I were one of her children, and she handed me a lamp to light the way to my room.

I was embarrassed for having made a fool of myself and felt like a six year old being sent off to bed. As soon as I put on some dry pajamas I got my diary from the drawer where I'd hidden it and sprawled on my cot to write in it.

Ordinarily I start from the beginning of the day and write down everything that's happened to me. But starting out from home with Papa and my suitcase seemed like something that happened three days ago. If I started from morning I would have filled the space for all five years. So I just began with the outdoor bath.

Suddenly heard a burglar coming! Nearly drowned and died of fright. Turned out to be an old man who lives in the barn. Am very curious to see

strange old man. Also Zenny's spirits! This is a
pretty weird place! Can I stand it for two weeks???
One month???

The old cot squeaked and squealed whenever I moved
and I missed my own bed at home. I needed something
comforting, remembered Mrs. Sugar's cookies, and ate
six, even though I'd already brushed my teeth.

5

IT WAS SUNDAY WHEN THE BAD THINGS
started to happen. I was still asleep that morning when
I felt cold water dripping on my forehead.

Good grief, I thought, Auntie Hata is wrong. The roof
does leak after all. I opened my eyes, and there was
Abu's face grinning over me.

"Get up! It's time to get up!" he yelled in my ear.

"You little monkey. You're worse than Joji!"

I tried to grab him by the neck, but he pulled away,
shrieking and laughing. I could hear him banging down
the steps yelling, "Rinko's up now, Ma."

It felt early, like maybe it was only six o'clock, so I
pulled the covers over my head to keep out the light. The
sheets felt rough and wrinkled, just the way Auntie
Hata's dresses looked.

I turned on my stomach and did my stretching exer-
cises, which I'd forgotten to do the night before. I'm
trying to catch up with Tami, who not only is prettier
than I am, but taller.

40

Mama tries to make me feel better by telling me I have good qualities that Tami doesn't have.

"Like what?" I ask.

And Mama will say something like, "Oh, you have a sweet nature, Rinko." But that's not much better than being told I have nice earlobes.

"Rinko! Get up! The first train's already gone, and Ma says the soup's ready." This time it was Zenny banging on my door.

The first time Zenny woke me up saying that, I thought I'd slept till noon and completely missed breakfast. But I discovered Auntie Hata makes soup every morning. Rice and *miso* soup. That's what we have every morning.

When I got down to the kitchen, I could smell the *miso* soup bubbling on the wood stove, and Auntie Hata was filling four bowls with steaming rice.

"Ah, you're just in time," she said.

I saw she was wearing another faded cotton dress even though it was Sunday. I guess if you don't go to church on Sundays, there's no need to get dressed up. Or maybe, I thought, she just didn't have any nice clothes.

I sort of missed Mama's long grace before we ate, but what I missed most was some hot cocoa and toast with lots of butter and jam. Sometimes on Sundays we even have pancakes, and I would've given my best red bead necklace for one pancake drowning in syrup.

But Auntie Hata said, "There's plenty of rice if you want more." She was spreading some chopped garlic on top of her rice and asked if I wanted some

"Nooo," I said, trying to hold my breath so I wouldn't smell it. "Do you always have rice and soup for breakfast?"

I was hoping she'd say no, that sometimes they had bacon and eggs and toast. But Zenny and Abu both nodded, and Auntie Hata told me that's what she'd had for breakfast since she was a child.

She was quiet for a minute and then said, "I wonder how she is?"

She was doing it again. Auntie Hata had this habit of saying whatever was rattling around in her head, whether it happened to fit into the conversation or not. No wonder people said she was odd, I thought. Probably nobody could ever figure out what she was talking about.

"Who?" I asked.

"My mother. She's still alive, you know, in Tamba Village."

She looked so lonesome then, I really felt sad for her. I'd never thought about Auntie Hata having a mother before. I only thought of her as Zenny and Abu's mother.

It seemed strange that a grown person like Auntie Hata could still miss her mama, who was thousands of miles away in a foreign land. But I guess Japan isn't a foreign land to her. It was her home. And I couldn't imagine how she'd had the courage to leave it and come so far away to marry Mr. Hata.

I was sitting there thinking my own thoughts, but Auntie Hata went on about her family, and I remembered Mama saying she needed company, so I tried hard to listen.

42

"You know my mother had ten children to raise, but still she planted and weeded and harvested the rice along with my father. By the time she was forty, her back was so bent, she couldn't straighten up."

"Why did she let you come so far? To America, I mean?"

"I guess she thought I'd have a better life here."

"Did you?"

Auntie Hata didn't exactly answer. She just said, "When I first came to America, I thought Mr. Hata was a banker. That's what he told our go-between."

Auntie Hata stopped and looked at me with a crooked smile. "He worked in a bank all right. But he swept the floors and never got near the money. When he lost that job, we moved to the valley and picked grapes and peaches."

"And that's when you sent Teru to Japan," Zenny said.

Auntie Hata looked wistful. "Yes, little Teru my first daughter. I sent her back to her grandmother because I couldn't care for her and work in the fields at the same time."

I was surprised. I didn't know Auntie Hata had another daughter who was still alive.

"She's nineteen now," Auntie Hata told me. "And when I have the money, I'm going to send for her. I really am."

Suddenly, she stopped talking as though I'd reached over and turned off a knob inside her head. She got me more soup and said, "We've got to fatten you up, Rinko. You're much too thin."

Abu ducked beneath the table to look at my legs.

"Yeah, she's got spindly spider legs," he announced.

"Thanks a lot, Abraham," I said.

The last thing I wanted was to get into a discussion about my skinny legs and how thin I was.

"What're we doing today?" I asked. "Picking more cucumbers?"

Zenny told me about the freight train that had jumped the tracks about a mile up the road and torn up a lot of ties. "They'll make real good firewood," he explained. "If we hurry, we can get some before everybody else does."

"Good," Auntie Hata said. "Rinko, go with them and see they don't get into any trouble."

"Like what?" I wanted to know what to watch out for.

But Auntie Hata was thinking about something else, and Zenny and Abu were already out the back door.

"Maybe the old man wants some firewood too," she called after them, and I could hear them hollering to the old man.

I was thinking I'd finally get to see him, but when I caught up with Zenny and Abu, they told me he'd already gotten some ties earlier that morning.

We must've walked almost an hour before we got to the place where the ties were torn out of the railbed. The railroad crews had tossed them to the side when they made the repairs, and already there were a dozen people scrambling for the good ones. They were dragging them into small carts or wagons like the one Zenny had brought along.

I wanted to plunge right in and get what we could, but Zenny motioned with his head to keep going. I guess he knew what he was doing because further on up the tracks, we found a pile of ties no one had discovered yet.

"Hey, these are good ones," Abu shouted.

He and Zenny were lifting a big one onto their wagon when I felt somebody come up behind us. I turned and saw a big man in dirty overalls. He had faded red hair and a scraggly beard and smelled of tobacco and liquor.

"Here, them ties is too big for you little Japs," he growled. "Move on down the tracks and get some scraps down there."

Abu edged away from the man, but Zenny clenched his fists and stuck out his chin.

"We got here first," he said. "These are ours."

I was amazed at how brave he was. I was so scared, my knees were knocking. I wanted to turn and run, but I could hear Auntie Hata telling me not to let the boys get into trouble. And if this wasn't trouble, I didn't know what was. I took a deep breath and yelled at the man.

"Leave them alone!"

I tried to yell as loud as I could, but my voice sounded small and squeaky, as if it came from a mouse in the ground.

The man turned for a minute and glared at me. "You stay outta this," he said. And he gave me a shove. That's when I got mad.

45

"You big bully," I yelled.

I was surprised at myself, but the words came from the pit of my stomach, where the core of my energy lives, according to Papa.

The big man was furious. He took a step toward me, ready to give me a swat, when Zenny charged at him, waving his fists and kicking.

I guess if Zenny was bigger, he might have had a chance. But the man was like a giant next to him. He shoved Zenny so hard, he fell over backwards and knocked Abu down. They were both sprawled on the ground, and I knew I'd be there next.

I tried frantically to remember what Cal had taught me about defending myself. I was ready to give the big man a hard kick in the shins when suddenly somebody reached from behind me and grabbed the man's wrist.

"*Yoi!*" a voice called. And before I knew it, the big man was flipped right over my head and was lying flat on the ground.

"Wow!" Abu yelled.

"Hey, old man!" Zenny hollered.

I whirled around and saw a tall Japanese man whose white hair was clipped so short it looked as though it had been cut with a lawnmower. He had a stern, thin face that looked as though it had forgotten how to smile. He was even taller than my brother Cal, who is almost six feet one, and he stood as straight as a telephone pole.

He glared at the man on the ground and watched him get to his feet, growling like a wounded bear. "Get out," he said. That was all, but I guess it was enough.

46

The big bully seemed to know the old man was nobody to mess with. He brushed himself off and slunk away without another word. I was really impressed.

The old man looked at each of us. "Are you all right?" he asked.

Since Zenny and Abu didn't have the manners to introduce me, I said, "My name is Rinko Tsujimura, and I've come to help Mrs. Hata for a while."

I expected the old man at least to say something pleasant, but all he did was give me a nod. He didn't even smile.

"I decided I could use more firewood after all," he said, as though he had to explain why he'd come. And without saying anything more, he began lifting ties onto Zenny's wagon.

6

•❦•

WHEN OUR WAGON WAS FULL, THE OLD
man said, "Well, I guess you don't need me any longer."

He put a hand on Zenny's shoulder. "Don't tell your
mama what happened. It'll just upset her, and she's got
enough to worry about as it is."

Then he gave Zenny and Abu a pat on the head, but he
just ignored me. In fact, I got the feeling he didn't like
me very much, and I felt the way I do when the white
girls at school ignore me.

But he's Japanese like me, I thought. Why doesn't he
like me? There was something strange and distant about
him.

He was keeping his distance, the way I do with some
people. For instance, I never talk first to a white person
because I might be ignored, and that really hurts. Maybe
that's how the old man felt about me, I thought.

"But if you talked to me, I'd like you back, old man,"
I said, as though he were there to hear me. "I wouldn't

48

ignore you if you'd just give me a chance. Why don't you—"

"Hey, Rinko, quit daydreaming." Zenny and Abu were heading for home and I had to run to catch up with them.

The old man was way ahead of us now, loping down the road with big graceful strides, like a long-legged giraffe, and pretty soon I couldn't even see him.

We were almost home when I heard a train coming from far down the tracks.

I saw Abu's face light up. "Hey, Zenny, here comes a freight."

"I hear it." Zenny sounded cautious, and he looked at me as though he wished I weren't there.

I knew in a minute what both of them were thinking. "You know what your mama said," I reminded them.

"You're not a snitch, are ya?" Zenny asked.

What could I say to a question like that? Nobody wants to be a snitch. Nobody in the world has any use for a snitch. Besides I didn't want to be rejected by Abu and Zenny as well as the old man. I thought things over for a minute and then said, "I won't tell if you show me how to ride the freights."

"You? You couldn't learn how."

"Bet I could."

"Bet ya a million billion dollars you can't," Abu piped up.

"You got a million billion dollars, Abu?" I asked.

"Sure. Got it buried in a hole in the ground."

49

"OK then," I said, surprising him. "I bet you a million billion dollars I can do it."

"Shake," he said.

But I wasn't about to be tricked again. I could be a good sport about it once, but not twice.

"It's a verbal agreement," I told him, and then I concentrated on Zenny.

"It ain't so easy," he began.

"Well, hurry up and tell me how."

Zenny frowned and I could see he still didn't want to tell me, but the freight train was closer now. The engine was chuffing and we could hear the squeal of the wheels on the tracks.

"Well, what ya do is run along the side of the car for a while, see. Then you reach for one of the grab bars. Then you gotta lift your feet up real quick on one of the lower bars and hold on tight. Then ya just ride till ya wanta get off."

"Gettin' off's the hard part," Abu admitted.

"It is?" It sounded like the easiest to me.

"Ya gotta be sure to jump in the direction the train's going," Zenny instructed. "Otherwise the wheels could roll right over ya and then, awwrrrrk, you're a goner."

He flicked his hand across his throat, made a terrible sound, and rolled his eyes.

"Yeah, awwrrrk!" Abu made an even more horrible sound and showed me the whites of his eyes.

They were trying to scare me, but it was too late to back down.

'Here it comes,'' Zenny shouted, and already Abu was

running ahead of him. Abu grabbed one of the bars, struggled to get his feet up, and then hung on for dear life, looking like a crab clinging to a boulder.

Zenny waited for the next car and then did exactly what he'd told me to do. All the time I was watching them, I could hear Auntie Hata's voice telling them not to ride the freight cars anymore. But I couldn't think about Auntie Hata for long because it was my turn, and if I didn't hurry, I'd miss the last car.

I ran along beside the boxcar, which wasn't hard because the train was going so slow. I reached up, grabbed the first bar I could, then swung my feet up, and there I was. I'd done it! I was riding along, clinging to the side of a boxcar. And it was the most fun I'd had in a long time.

"Hey, look at me!" I yelled, as though my brother Joji were standing there looking envious.

Mama would have been horrified. "That's not ladylike, Rinko," she would have said. "And besides, it's dangerous. Get off at once."

I was surprised at myself for enjoying it so much. Here I was behaving like my ten-and-a-half-year-old brother instead of his older sister. But that's how I am. I am very easily influenced by whoever I happen to be with, and ever since I got to East Oakland, I'd been behaving more and more like Zenny and Abu.

On the other hand, when I'm with my friend Tami, I behave the way she does and think about boys and getting married, which is what her mother is so interested in— matching people up, that is. She's always trying to find wives for the bachelors who live in the church dormitory, and when my widowed Aunt Waka came to visit from Japan, she spent the entire summer trying to find a husband for her.

Anyway, Tami always asks me about my brother Cal's friends. She wants to know how old they are and whether they have girl friends and whether I think they're good-looking. Next to my brother Cal, I think she likes Hisashi best because he's got such pretty eyes. The reason I like him is because everybody calls him Hy, and I just love saying "Hi, Hy!" to him.

Actually I guess I am about five different people depending on who I'm with. With Joji I can be mean and bossy. With Mama and Papa I can be stubborn and ornery. With Mrs. Sugar I can be cheerful and sweet. And with the big bully, I really tried to be strong and brave, the way my Aunt Waka told me to be.

The trouble is, I can't seem to stay that way. The minute I get to school, I am Rinko, the meek and mild, and I don't like myself much when I'm like that. In fact, I never feel like my own true self at school. But sometimes I'm not exactly sure which *is* the real true me.

I guess I'm always changing, never the same. But Mrs. Sugar once told me that's only natural. She said, "Different people bring out different qualities in us, Rinko. Sometimes we behave the way people expect us to, not the way we really want to." And I got to thinking maybe I feel clumsy and homely when I'm with Tami because she *expects* me to be that way.

52

Mrs. Sugar and I have some very philosophical discussions, and I was wondering what she'd make of the old man and how he'd treated me. I was wishing I could run through the hole in our hedge right now and tell her about him.

Then I heard Zenny yell, "Gettin' off!"

And he jumped off, running in the direction the train was going.

Then Abu yelled, "Gettin' off!" and he turned a couple of somersaults away from the tracks when he jumped.

I took a deep breath and yelled, "Here I come!"

I tried to jump, but my fingers were clenched so tight around the grab bar, I couldn't seem to let go.

"Jump, Rinko!"

"Get off! Get off! Let go!"

"I'm coming!"

I took a deep breath, closed my eyes, let go, and jumped. I heard the wheels of the train click by practically in front of my nose as I fell to the ground. And then I felt a sharp pain in my ankle.

Zenny and Abu came running up to me.

"I *told* you to jump the way the train was going."

"Boy, you nearly got yourself killed."

I wanted to tell them I tried to do it right, but all I could do was moan.

"I think I sprained my ankle," I finally said. I tried to get up, but a streak of red hot pain shot right to the tip of my head. "Ouch!" I yelled.

I felt awful. Here I was supposed to be such a help and comfort to Auntie Hata, and I'd not only let Zenny and Abu ride the freights, which she expressly forbade them to do, but I'd done it myself. Furthermore, I had gotten hurt by being clumsy and dumb and behaving like a ten year old. It seemed a bad omen, and I had the feeling my two weeks in East Oakland were going to be an utter disaster.

"Now what're we gonna do?" Abu asked. He looked at me as though he wished I'd just disappear into a hole in the ground.

But Zenny helped me up and told me to see if I could walk.

I tested my ankle, gritted my teeth, and said, "I can walk."

I don't know how I did it, but I managed to hobble after Zenny as he pulled his wagon of wood home. And the closer I got to the house, the worse I felt.

"What am I going to tell your mama?" I asked.

"We won't snitch," Zenny offered.

"But she'll see my ankle."

"The old man'll fix it."

"Yeah, he'll make ya eat ground-up snake," Abu added.

"Aw, cut it out, Abu," Zenny said. "Rinko's feeling bad."

And I most certainly was. My ankle throbbed and felt like a balloon.

"You don't eat ground-up snake for sprained ankles,"

I said to Abu. "That cure's only for little boys who don't listen to their mamas."

"Oh, yeah?"

"Yeah."

It's a good thing we got to the barn just then because I was picking a fight with a little eight year old, just the way I do with my brother Joji. My only excuse was that my ankle really hurt.

The barn door creaked as Zenny pulled it open, and we trooped in single file, me last.

"We need help," Zenny called out to the old man.

And from somewhere deep inside the barn I heard the old man answer, "What, again?"

7

I WAS NEVER SO SURPRISED AS WHEN I
limped into that old barn. I was expecting a dusty, dirty
placed filled with cobwebs and smelling like horses. Instead, it was like walking inside one of those kaleido-
scopes you hold up and turn to make wonderful colored
designs.

The barn was filled with huge, bright-colored kites
hanging from the rafters and the hayloft and wherever
there was space on the walls. I just stood there for a
minute looking around, with my mouth open, forgetting
all about my ankle.

I could see an enormous butterfly kite with yellow-
and-black wings, a bird kite with blue and purple feath-
ers, an orange, bug-eyed cicada with folded wings,
rectangular kites with glaring samurai warrior faces,
armless *daruma* dolls, vassal kites with arms like air-
plane wings, and even a centipede kite that must have
been six feet long.

56

When I finally stopped staring and closed my mouth, I saw the old man. He was sitting at a table, next to a narrow metal cot, wearing old baggy clothes and a cloth band twisted around his forehead. He was painting a samurai face on a large piece of diamond-shaped paper and scarcely seemed to notice us.

The table was filled with pots of brushes, paste, and bright-colored paints. I saw the old man put a brush into his mouth and thought for a minute he was eating paint. But he was just bringing the tip of the brush to a point so he could paint in the eyes.

"Hey, you making a new kite?" Zenny asked, bending for a closer look.

The old man put out an arm to keep Zenny from jarring his elbow.

"Don't touch my arm when I'm painting," he warned. And he brushed in two round black eyeballs inside a pair of wide, oval, white eyes.

Abu giggled as the samurai glared cross-eyed and the old man painted in two enormous bushy eyebrows, slanting them toward a big nose with flaring nostrils.

"He's glaring at his mortal enemy," the old man explained. "The eyes show he is concentrating, as he is about to deliver the fatal blow with his sword. *Yoi!*"

I jumped when the old man yelled. It was as though he had become the samurai he was painting. I didn't mean to say anything, but when I shifted the weight onto my sore foot by mistake, it just slipped out. "Ouch!" I groaned.

The old man put down his brush and looked at me. First at my face scrunched up in pain and then at my right foot, which sort of dangled, with only the tip of my toe touching the ground. I felt like an old stork.

"So, you've been riding the freights, have you?" His dark eyes were stern.

I wondered how he knew. I didn't think anybody had seen us.

"Well, uh, sort of."

"Sort of?"

"Well, I guess, yes. It was my first time."

"I thought as much." The old man sniffed. "They all twist their ankles the first time."

"You mean Zenny and Abu did too?"

"Certainly. Both of them. And more than once."

No wonder they knew where to bring me for help.

The old man motioned for me to sit on a chair, and he knelt to examine my foot. I was surprised how gentle he was when he took off my shoe and sock and felt my ankle with both hands.

"Is it broke?" Abu wanted to know. "Is the bone sticking out?"

But my question was, "Will I have to go to the hospital?" Already I could see myself with a huge cast on my leg, hobbling on crutches for the rest of the summer.

Zenny asked, "Is it a bad sprain?"

The old man didn't answer any of us. He sent Zenny out for a bucket of cold water and emptied some leaves from his teapot into it. Then he scooped up the wet leaves, put them carefully on my ankle, and wrapped a towel around it. He propped my foot up on an old apple crate and told me to sit still for a while.

"It will soon feel better," he said. "It's not a bad sprain."

He was right. The cold tea leaves felt good on my swollen ankle and before long the pain gradually eased up.

"Thanks a lot," I said. I was so relieved I wouldn't have to see a doctor.

The old man was certainly an improvement over Dr. Oniki, who comes to see me when I'm really sick, like the times I had measles and chicken pox. He smells of camphor and gags me with a tongue depressor and then asks me a lot of questions.

"How cah I tahk wi thith i mah mouf?" I have to ask.

Once, when I had the stomach flu, he gave me some horrible brown stuff that Joji called earthworm juice. It tasted worse than biting into a green persimmon, but Mama said, "Good medicine tastes bad, Rinko, just as good advice hurts your ears." Mama is full of sayings like that.

I'll let Mama try any of her home remedies before I let her call Dr. Oniki. The one that works is her treatment for colds. What I have to do is soak my feet in a bucket of almost boiling hot water for twenty minutes and then for one minute in icy cold. My feet come out looking like boiled lobsters, I'm dripping with sweat, and Mama then rushes me into bed. I guess all that scares off any bugs, because the next morning I usually feel better.

Well, the minute the old man finished taking care of my ankle, he went back to work on his kite. He fitted his painting carefully onto a kite frame and then pasted the edges over the guideline string.

"You know, a kite is an extension of life," he said, as though he were talking to the samurai on his kite. "It lets you become part of the sky. You become the kite and the sky and the universe itself, and then we are all one and the same."

I wasn't exactly sure what he meant, but I tried to look as though I understood.

Zenny and Abu didn't even pretend. They just told the old man they were almost finished with their new kite.

"Well then, what are you waiting for?" the old man asked. "Go finish it. There's a thermal today and we should get a good lift."

"OK. See ya in the fields after lunch," Zenny said.

And he scrambled out of the barn without giving me another thought. Abu was right behind him.

"Hey, Abu," I yelled. "What about the million billion dollars you owe me?"

But he was gone, and if the old man thought that was a strange question for me to be hollering at Abu, he didn't show it. He was busy knitting small strips of cloth to make a tail for his kite and almost seemed to have forgotten I was there.

I cleared my throat to remind him. He looked very

wise, as if he knew a lot of things, and I was dying to get his opinion about the spirits in the fields. I also wanted to know if he thought Auntie Hata was really crazy, the way people said. I wanted him to talk to me. I wanted him to like me. But first, I had to get his attention.

"I can wiggle my ears," I said. "It's my best talent."

And I pushed back my hair and wiggled them so he'd see how clever I was to use muscles most people don't even know they have. I am the only one in my family who can do this, and it just about kills Joji that he can't. He would dearly love to learn how, but it's something I can't possibly teach him. You can either do it or you can't.

Although I was showing him my wonderful and unique talent, the old man didn't even look up. He just asked, "Where did you say you were from?"

"Berkeley."

"And what do your parents do?"

"Well, my mama has a home laundry in our basement," I began. "She opened it last year to help Papa pay his bills, since he wasn't making enough money with his barber shop. But Papa isn't a barber anymore. He's got this repair shop in our garage because he's good at fixing things up. Mostly he repairs cars because he's such a good mechanic."

I went on to tell him about my big brother, Cal, who was in Alaska earning tuition money for the university and about my little brother, Joji, who is the same age as Zenny but looks more like Abu.

I was blabbing as though I'd never stop and had just

started to tell him about my friend Tami and our neighbor Mrs. Sugar, when the old man stopped me.

"Do your mother and father go to the Japanese church?"

I had the feeling the old man would like me better if I said no, but how could I do that when Mama was a pillar of the church and God was her best friend? So I didn't say anything. Sometimes that works when you don't want to answer a question. But I guess the old man was too smart not to know what I was up to. The next thing he said was so strange, I couldn't understand it.

He said, "Well, you may tell your parents about me if you wish. But you are to tell no one else. Especially your white neighbor or the minister of your church."

"You mean Mrs. Sugar? And Reverend Mitaka? How come?"

"I have my reasons," the old man said mysteriously.

Then he got up as though he'd finished with me and my ankle. He unwrapped the towel and removed the tea leaves.

"You can go now," he said. "Keep your foot elevated and put more cold compresses on it if it hurts."

I still had a million questions I wanted to ask him. I'd poured out practically my whole life to him, but he hadn't told me a single thing about himself. I started to open my mouth, but he dismissed me with a wave of his hand, as though he was letting me go after keeping me in from recess. He'd turned cold and distant again, and I could feel the chill even in my sore ankle.

I tried to think of something nice to say as I limped out.

"Did you know samurai kites bring good luck to their makers?" I asked.

To tell the honest truth, I only made that up just then, but I thought maybe it would make him feel more kindly toward me. If it did, he certainly didn't show it. He just went back to tying the flying line to his kite as though I'd already gone.

8

•–•··•–•·•

I KNEW TURNING MY ANKLE WAS A BAD
omen. Mama always says bad things happen in threes,
so I knew I probably had two more coming. Or maybe, I
thought, coming to East Oakland was the first bad thing
and I was already on my second one.

Sometimes when two bad things happen, Mama will
purposely break something she doesn't care about and
say, "There! That's the third bad thing. Now we're
finished."

I wished I could get my two more bad things over
with fast, but I certainly couldn't break any of Auntie
Hata's dishes. She didn't have that many to spare.

What really made me feel so awful about the whole
thing was that Auntie Hata didn't get mad when I told her
what I'd done. What she said was, "Ah, well, Rinko, I
guess you're still only a child after all."

And she put cold compresses on my ankle and kept me
off my feet, which made me feel worse than if she'd

gotten mad and scolded me for being so stupid. Mama might just as well have sent Joji, I thought, for all the help I was to Auntie Hata.

As soon as my ankle was better, I tried to make up for everything and be a more responsible person. I was still limping, but I could help Auntie Hata hang out her wash, which she scrubbed in a big metal tub heated on the wood stove. And I ironed her sheets and pillowcases so she'd have nice smooth sheets to sleep on. I could see why she usually didn't bother and why her clothes looked wrinkled. Ironing wasn't easy when you had to heat a big heavy iron on the wood stove.

I also swept out the whole house, which wasn't hard since there were no rugs, and I used damp tea leaves to keep down the dust. It didn't matter what day I cleaned, because Auntie Hata didn't have a special day for it like Mama, who wants it done on Saturdays. Auntie Hata seemed to do things when the spirit moved her, and that was fine with me.

One morning I got up even before the first train to help with breakfast. Actually, what I wanted to do was ask Auntie Hata about the old man before Zenny and Abu came down.

I saw she already had a pot of rice bubbling on the stove and was poking at the fire, talking to it so it would burn brighter.

"Shall I help make the soup?" I asked.

"That would be nice," Auntie Hata said into the fire. "I'll go out and get some fresh cucumbers."

And before I could even say, "old man," she was out the back door and gone.

The next thing I knew, she was calling to me.

"Rinko, Rinko! Hurry! Come quick!"

I was sure something awful had happened, like maybe she'd come across a snake out in the fields. I grabbed a knife and ran out, ready to stab the snake if I had to. But Auntie Hata was just standing there, smiling and pointing.

"Look, Rinko, it's been raining spiders."

Sure enough, there were tiny spiders and wispy webs all over the fields and the morning dew was caught in them like tiny crystal beads. It was the prettiest thing.

"Will the spiders eat the cucumbers?" I asked.

"Not likely. They'll probably all be blown off somewhere by the wind and be gone by tomorrow." Auntie Hata bent down for a closer look at the shimmery webs and said, "What a shame."

I knew exactly what she meant. I think it's awful that spiders work so hard spinning beautiful lacy webs—so neat and perfect—only to have them destroyed in a second by the wind or some giant human being.

Auntie Hata picked her cucumbers carefully so she wouldn't destroy any of the webs. And I guess that's when I began to like her, because that's exactly what I would have done. That is also when I smelled something burning.

"It's the rice!" I yelled.

When Auntie Hata and I got back to the house, the

kitchen was filled with smoke, and Zenny and Abu were standing there yelling, "Fire! Fire! The stove's on fire!"

"It's only the rice," I hollered, and I flapped a dish towel to get rid of the smoke, while Auntie Hata grabbed the pot from the stove.

By the time we sat down to have our soup and some of the rice we saved from the top of the pot, I'd given up trying to have a private conversation with Auntie Hata. I just blurted out my question in front of Zenny and Abu.

"What's wrong with the old man, anyway?" I asked. "He's so strange and unfriendly." And I told what he'd said about not mentioning him to Mrs. Sugar or our minister.

Auntie Hata stopped eating and looked at me thoughtfully. Then she said, "He's had some hard times." As though that would explain everything.

"Like what?"

I could tell Auntie Hata was thinking carefully what to say, like Papa when he rubs his mustache.

"It's not always easy to make a life for yourself in a strange land," she said. "Sometimes . . . often, you're afraid, and you close yourself off and shut people out."

I could understand that. I've felt that way myself lots of times even if I'm *not* in a strange land. But I wondered why the old man should be afraid of me or my friends?

"Aw, the old man ain't afraid of nothing," Zenny said.

"He sure ain't," Abu agreed.

But Auntie Hata didn't seem to hear them. "We all get scared sometimes," she said. "And lonely too. Oh, yes. Lonely lots of times."

"Well, you don't have to be lonely while I'm here," I reminded her.

Auntie Hata smiled, crinkling her eyes into two small crescent moons. "That's right, Rinko."

She reached over to pat my shoulder and then got up to clear the table, and I still didn't know a thing about the old man.

The second bad thing happened when I'd almost forgotten about the first one. It was a lot worse than my sprained ankle, and it didn't happen to me.

It happened just as we were going to take more cucumbers to the factory. We had loaded up the truck and were ready to leave when an old beat-up truck came rattling along, and I heard a sound like the honking of a tired goose.

I knew what it was when I saw the canvas flapping over the sides of the truck and a scale dangling in the back. It looked just like the truck of a Japanese peddler who comes to our house once a week on Thursday afternoons.

His truck is filled with crates of carrots and string beans, taro root and long white radish, ginger and burdock root, and gallon tins of bean curd squares floating in water. There are also hundred-pound sacks of white rice and barrels of soy sauce and tubs of yellow pickled radish. Everything in the truck smells awful and wonderful at the same time and makes my mouth water.

A smiling, skinny Japanese man jumped out of this truck and Auntie Hata called to him. "You're exactly the person I wanted to see, Mr. Kogi. I'm all out of bean curd cakes, and I need a sack of rice."

She hurried into the house to get a pan for the bean curd cakes, and that was when I heard the freight train coming.

Zenny and Abu took a quick look at each other and yelled, "We'll be right back."

I knew exactly what they were up to. "You'd better not!" I said. "You'd better come back right now."

But they completely ignored me, and I couldn't go after them because the peddler was talking to me. He twisted the cover off a small jar of pink grease and poked it under my nose.

"Here, smell," he said. "It's hair pomade made by my missus. It comes in three different scents."

I took a sniff and said, "Strawberry," as if I was taking a smelling test.

"That's right," he said. "Want to try some?"

He was smiling and waiting, and I could see the gold fillings in his front teeth. I didn't want to hurt his feelings, but I certainly didn't want to put that pink grease on my hair and go around smelling like strawberries. Auntie Hata came back just in time to rescue me.

"Oh, is that more of your hair pomade?" she asked,

69

and she took a big dab with her finger, bent over, and smeared it all over her shoes.

"It's much better than shoe polish," she said, laughing, "and I have the best smelling shoes in East Oakland."

The peddler laughed too. I guess he didn't really care whether Auntie Hata used his pomade on her head or her feet.

She didn't have enough money to pay for the rice, but the peddler heaved the big sack on his shoulder and carried it into the kitchen for her.

"Pay me next time," he said, and he rattled off in his noisy truck.

Auntie Hata looked around for Zenny and Abu. "Now where did those two rascals go?"

"I know," I said. "I'll go get them." And I left Auntie Hata cranking up the truck's motor.

I ran out the front gate and headed toward the slight rise, just before the freight train started down the slope. The train rolled by as I got there, and just as I thought, Zenny and Abu were hitching a ride. Abu was on the front ladder of one car and Zenny on the back.

"Get off!" I yelled. "We're leaving."

"OK," Zenny hollered back.

"Right now!" I shouted.

So Zenny jumped, landed on his feet and ran hard until he got his balance.

Abu turned to wave at me.

"Get off! Get off!" I yelled.

70

But he didn't. He was looking back at me instead of where he should jump. And when he finally did jump, he fell to the ground and rolled backwards toward the wheels of the train.

"Watch out!" Zenny hollered.

"Stop!" I screamed at the train. But it kept right on going, and I thought I saw a wheel roll over Abu's arm before he could roll away.

I heard somebody screaming like crazy but didn't know it was me. Abu had rolled away from the tracks, but his right arm was twisted, as if it didn't belong to his body, and there was blood and grease and dirt all over it. His glasses lay smashed on the ground beside him.

I was still screaming when I got to him, and Zenny yelled, "Stop screaming, Rinko."

But I saw Abu all crumpled up on the ground, and I couldn't stop.

"Abu's dead!" I screamed. "Abu's dead! Abu's dead!"

9

•⚬•⚬••⚬•⚬••⚬•⚬••⚬•⚬••⚬•⚬••⚬•⚬••⚬•⚬••⚬•⚬••⚬•⚬••⚬•⚬••⚬•⚬••⚬•⚬••⚬•⚬••⚬•⚬••⚬•⚬••⚬•⚬••⚬•⚬••⚬•

AUNTIE HATA MUST'VE HEARD ME, BE-
cause all of a sudden she was next to me and Zenny. She
cried out when she saw Abu and knelt down beside him.

"Abu Chan, Abu Chan. *Doshita? Doshita?* What happened?" she murmured over and over. She felt his head
and touched his cheek and tried to check his pulse.

"I'm sorry, Ma. I'm sorry," Zenny sobbed. Tears were
streaming down his face.

I was crying too and still screaming, "Abu's dead!"

He was so still, with no color in his face. His eyes
were closed and his arm was twisted and horrible looking.

"Stop screaming, Rinko," Auntie Hata said to me in
a firm voice. "Abu is going to be all right, but we've got
to get him to a hospital quickly."

She took a handkerchief from her pocket and tied it
around Abu's arm to stop the bleeding. Then she picked
him up carefully and carried him to the truck. Zenny and

72

I trailed after her, sobbing and crying. She told us to get in the truck first, and then she lifted Abu onto our laps.

I could see she didn't want to let go of him, but she had to drive, so she put Abu's head and shoulders on my lap and stretched his legs over Zenny's. I was surprised how heavy he was. I could feel my heart pounding all over my body and I felt awful about all the mean things I'd said to Abu. I didn't know if he could hear me, but I talked to him.

"It's OK, Abu. You're going to be OK. You'll see." I felt as though he'd stay alive as long as he could hear me talking to him. So I talked all the way to the hospital. And Zenny kept patting his legs.

I don't know how Auntie Hata got to Highland Hospital so fast. I guess she knew the way because she'd taken Mr. Hata there to see the doctor, even though he hated the place.

As soon as we got there, the doctors rushed Abu into the emergency room, and Auntie Hata and Zenny and I waited in the corridor outside.

I guess I feel about hospitals the way Mr. Hata did— that once you're stuck in one, you're going to come out in a wooden box. I kept wishing we could hurry up and get Abu out of that awful place. Well, after a while the doctor came and told us they were taking Abu to surgery.

We all jumped up from the bench, and I yelled, "Surgery! You mean you're going to cut off his arm?"

"Oh, please, no!" Auntie Hata cried.

73

But the doctor told us not to worry, that they'd take good care of Abu, and that we should just sit down and wait.

I guess we must've sat there in that crowded hallway for a couple of hours, with nobody paying any attention to us. I felt as though an egg beater was churning up my stomach and everything else all together. And I guess Auntie Hata felt the same way, because she kept twisting a handkerchief in her hands until it was almost in shreds. Every once in a while she would send Zenny to go ask somebody about Abu.

"What's happening to my brother?" he'd ask anybody in a white uniform.

And whoever he talked to would just say something like, "Everything's OK, sonny. Don't worry. Go sit down till your doctor comes to talk to you."

So we sat and waited and waited and waited, and by then I felt all ground up like the sesame seeds in Mama's mortar. When I went to look at a clock, it was almost six o'clock.

Finally a doctor came out and called, "Mrs. Hata?"

Auntie Hata shot up from the bench as if she'd exploded from a cannon. She had a hard time finding the right words to ask the doctor what she wanted to know. "My boy, he's OK? He's OK? Please?"

"Your boy has lost a lot of blood but we gave him a transfusion," the doctor said slowly. "There's been some nerve damage, and he may not regain full use of his right arm. But he's holding his own. You can go see him now in Ward C."

74

Auntie Hata was trying hard to understand, but she wasn't sure. "Abu's OK?" she asked me over and over. "He's OK?"

I wasn't sure myself. All I could say was, "I think so, Auntie Hata."

We found our way to Ward C, and there was Abu in a big room filled with a lot of sick people. He was in a corner bed and he looked small and helpless with his arm bandaged clear up to his shoulder. He was asleep and couldn't talk to us, but Auntie Hata wouldn't leave him.

"You know the way to the old man's Eagle Cafe?" she asked Zenny.

"I can find it."

"Well, you and Rinko walk there and tell him what happened. Wait until he gets off work. Then take the streetcar home with him."

She took two nickles from her coin purse and gave one to each of us for carfare. She said she wanted to be there when Abu woke up and didn't know when she'd get home.

"Rinko, can you make some supper for the two of you?"

I nodded. We could always have cucumbers with soy sauce and pour hot tea over the rice left over from breakfast. I didn't want to leave Auntie Hata there by herself, but she didn't look scared or frightened anymore. She was calm and strong, the way the old man had been the day he chased off the bully at the railroad tracks.

"Go on now," she said, and she nudged us toward the door. There certainly wasn't anything vague about Auntie

Hata then. She took charge as though she knew exactly what to do.

I guess Zenny and I must've walked about thirty blocks to The Eagle Cafe. My knees ached and one big toe throbbed, but I was too worried about Abu to think about myself. I felt it was my fault that Abu was lying in the hospital half dead. If only I'd stopped him before he rode that freight, I thought.

I knew Zenny was feeling as bad as I was, because he didn't say one word all the way to Seventh Street. We just plodded along like two strangers, each of us bundled up in our own gloomy thoughts.

When we finally got to The Eagle Cafe, we found the old man frying some potatoes at the grill. He was wearing a white apron and chef's hat, and he was so surprised to see us, he just froze with the egg turner clutched in his hand.

"Zenny! Rinko! What are you doing here?"

That was when Zenny and I both started talking, and I felt as though I was drowning in all the words that came tumbling out of my mouth. Between the two of us, we told the old man everything that had happened.

"And Abu? How is he now?" the old man asked when we finally stopped.

"The doctor said he had nerve damage," I said. "He's lost a lot of blood. Maybe . . . maybe he's going to die." I began to cry again.

For a minute the old man didn't know what to do with us. Then he went to talk to a bald-headed white man in

76

a rumpled gray sweater who was sitting at the cash register. He called him Mr. Sabatini, and I guess he was the owner of the cafe. When the old man came back, he told us to sit down at the counter and he'd make us something to eat.

"I get off soon," he said, "and by the time you finish eating, I'll be ready to go home with you."

Then the old man was making toast, breaking eggs on the grill, and frying two ham steaks and some potatoes. It was like the time I'd seen him painting the samurai on his kite. His hands were steady and sure and knew exactly what to do without the old man's even having to think about it. I never saw anybody cook so fast. And suddenly everything was there in front of me, hot and sizzling, on a thick white plate, and it smelled so wonderful I nearly fainted.

Zenny and I pitched in and ate as though we hadn't seen any food for three weeks. It was strange eating breakfast for supper, but I'd been eating lunch for breakfast every day at Auntie Hata's, and it didn't seem to make any difference to my stomach. I sopped up all the runny egg yolk with my toast and ate every bit of the ham and potatoes.

The old man kept an eye on us while he served some other customers, and for dessert he gave each of us a piece of apple pie. He also poured a little coffee into our milk, and I had two glasses.

When it was time to go, the old man tried to pay Mr. Sabatini, but he wouldn't take his money.

"Forget it, Manki," he said. "It's on the house." I thought he'd called him monkey.

"He called you Manki," Zenny said as soon as we were outside. "That ain't your name, is it?"

The old man shook his head. "Maybe someday he will take the trouble to call me by my proper name, Manki-chi," he said, and he strode so fast toward the corner to catch the streetcar, Zenny and I had to run to keep up.

The streetcar rattled and poked along until it finally reached the end of the line, and then we still had about a mile to walk to get home.

It was really spooky walking along that dark road with only the empty fields stretching out around us. I was dying to hold a friendly hand, but nobody offered me one, so I hugged myself real hard instead. I also kept watching for spirits in case there were any hovering around in the weeds.

I guess Zenny knew what I was doing because he said, "They ain't there tonight."

In a way that made me feel worse, because then I wondered if maybe the spirits were at the hospital waiting to take Abu to the spirit world. I thought maybe Abu's papa was there that minute, trying to take Abu with him.

"No!" I yelled into the dark fields. "You can't take him."

Zenny gave me a funny look, but I guess he was used to having his mama pop out with strange remarks. The old man turned to look at me too, but he didn't say anything either.

The old man came home with us, and we all sat in the kitchen waiting for Auntie Hata. The old man asked Zenny about his kite, and I was beginning to feel left out again when Auntie Hata finally came home. I took one look at her face and knew something terrible had happened.

"What is it, Mrs. Hata?" the old man asked. "Is it Abu?"

"No, no, Abu is all right. He's asleep and the doctor made me leave. But it's gone!"

"What is, Ma?"

"The truck. Our truck's gone!"

"The truck? The truck's gone?" I asked like an echo.

The old man made Auntie Hata sit down and told her to calm herself. "Are you sure you just didn't forget where you parked it?"

"No, no. I left it right by the entrance."

"That's right," I said remembering. We'd pulled up at the emergency entrance and piled out without giving the truck another thought.

"And you left the keys in it?" Zenny asked.

Auntie Hata nodded sadly. "The keys, the cucumbers, the truck . . . somebody's taken them all."

"Maybe somebody parked it for you," I said hopefully.

"I walked around that hospital three times looking for it," Auntie Hata said, shaking her head. "It's gone. Somebody's stolen our truck!"

There it was, I thought, feeling terrible. That was the third bad thing to happen. My ankle, Abu's accident, and now the truck. Things seemed to be going from bad to worse ever since I arrived, and I began to feel like a jinx on Auntie Hata's life.

"I'll call Papa. He'll think of something." I started to get up and then remembered there was no phone in the house and that I'd have to wait until the next day to call from the hospital.

"I'll speak to the cop who comes to The Eagle for coffee every morning," the old man said. "Maybe he can help you find your truck."

But nothing we said could cheer her up. "I can't earn a living without the truck," Auntie Hata said miserably.

She let out a low moan, as though all the energy was drifting out of her body, like air going out of a balloon.

"We're finished, old man," she said slowly. "I think we're finished."

10

AS SOON AS I CALLED MAMA AND PAPA
the next day, they rushed over to the hospital. And they
brought Reverend Mitaka with them. He is a bachelor,
who Tami's mother is dying to find a wife for, and he
is so shy, he never looks up from his notes when he
preaches. He also has bad eyes and wears such thick
glasses he looks a little like an owl.

I wished Mama hadn't brought him, but I guess she
thought he could comfort Auntie Hata. Or maybe she
thought Abu would get better if he prayed over him. I
was sincerely hoping he wouldn't, but Reverend Mitaka
prayed all right. He put his hand on Abu's forehead,
and we stood around his bed as if we were having a
prayer meeting.

I was so embarrassed because everybody in the ward
was staring at us. I kept my eyes open all the time,
watching to see if Abu would open his, but he didn't.
Zenny had his eyes open too and was making circles on
the floor with his left toe.

When I was feeling like I wanted to sink right into the floor, Reverend Mitaka finally stopped, and Auntie Hata took him and Mama and Papa aside to tell them about Abu's arm.

Zenny and I tried to get Abu to open his eyes.

"Hey, Abu, it's me," Zenny said, bending close to his ear. "You OK?"

Abu's eyelids flickered and he managed a small smile.

"Yeah," he said in a thin voice. He sounded as though he was inside a tunnel. "Next time I'll jump better."

"Next time nothing," I said, sounding like his mother. "You'd better stick to flying kites."

The minute I said that I could have choked myself for being so stupid. How was Abu going to fly a kite if he couldn't use his right hand?

"Listen, Abu," I said, changing the subject as fast as I could. "You don't have to pay me that million billion dollars you still owe me. OK?"

That made Abu grin a little bit. "OK. Shake," he said, and he stuck the fingers of his left hand out from under the covers. They felt hot and weak, and Abu couldn't even give my hand a squeeze.

I couldn't stand seeing him look so pathetic. "Listen, I'll bring your turtle, Herbert, to see you next time. OK?" I said, and I left in a hurry to go see what Mama and Papa were talking about. They were discussing Auntie Hata's truck.

"Let me look around," Papa said. "Maybe I can find another old truck and fix it up for you."

But Auntie Hata just shook her head. "What's the

use?" she said. "Summer's almost over and the cucumbers will soon be gone. Then what will I do? I can't do gardening the way Mr. Hata used to. No, I don't need another truck. All I want is for Abu to get well."

"He will, Mrs. Hata," Mama said. "He will."

When it was time to leave, Mama took me aside. "Well, Rinko," she said. "Your two weeks are about up. Do you want to come home with us or will you stay until the end of the month?"

I was surprised she should even ask, but I guess she did it to make me realize what I'd already decided. I hadn't even thought about going home early.

"I can't leave," I said to Mama. "Auntie Hata *really* needs me now."

Mama put her arm around me and gave me a hard squeeze. "Good," she said. "I hoped you'd say that."

Papa checked with me too. "You're sure you're all right?" he asked. "You're sure you want to stay?"

"Sure, Papa," I said. "I've got some unfinished business in East Oakland."

Papa looked puzzled, but I couldn't tell him I had to stay to find out what was bothering the old man. And I didn't admit the real reason I wanted to stay, which was that I'd grown to like Auntie Hata. In fact, I liked her a lot.

Auntie Hata went to the hospital every morning to stay with Abu and didn't get home until suppertime. It took her an hour to get there on the streetcar, and I kept wishing Reverend Mitaka or Mama would hurry up and produce a miracle so her truck would turn up. But they didn't.

"It's my own fault for being so stupid," Auntie Hata said. "*Shikataganai*. It can't be helped. I hope the truck is happy wherever it is."

She talked about the truck as if it were a person. In fact, she told me that she believed everything—even a plant or a chair—had a soul of its own.

It seemed like a good time to ask about those spirit lights, so I asked, "What about the souls of the dead? Do you think they really come back? Have you seen them out in the fields?"

Auntie Hata shook her head. "No, I haven't seen them," she answered, "but that doesn't mean they're not there."

"What about your little girls and Mr. Hata? Are their spirits still around?"

Auntie Hata didn't answer right away. "What I think is, if a person believes in the spirits, then they're there."

It wasn't exactly yes, but it wasn't no either. Maybe, I thought, if I really and truly believed in the spirits, then I'd see them. I still wasn't sure.

Every evening when the old man got home from work, he stopped by to ask about Abu. Each time Zenny and I would ask if his policeman friend had found the truck. But the old man would shake his head and say, "Not yet. Not yet."

In the meantime, the cucumbers were getting big and

fat and going crazy wanting to be picked. I was getting like Auntie Hata and could almost hear them saying, "Pick us! Please pick us!" So Zenny and I kept stuffing them into sacks even if there was no way to get them to the factory.

One day Zenny and I made a roadside stand and put up a sign saying, "Fresh cucumbers. 3 for 5¢" But only one lady stopped. She bought six and gave us a dime, and that was all we earned the whole day.

The next day we picked some of the blackberries that grew wild at the edge of the fields and tried selling them with the cucumbers. But that day nobody stopped. Not one single person. So Zenny and I ate most of the blackberries ourselves and ended up with horrible-looking purple teeth. It was all very discouraging, and personally, I felt as if I never wanted to see another blackberry or cucumber again in my whole entire life.

On Saturday Papa came out to help us take some cucumbers to the factory. But when he checked our sacks, he discovered most of the cucumbers had shriveled up in the heat and some had even begun to rot.

"What a shame," he kept saying. "Such a waste." There was nothing we could do except throw them out.

Zenny and I felt awful, but Auntie Hata didn't seem to care. "Let them rot," she said. "It doesn't matter."

Ever since Abu's accident, nothing mattered to her except Abu. She didn't care about the cucumbers, and she didn't care about herself. She wore the same wrinkled dress every day and stopped polishing her shoes with strawberry hair pomade. And she hardly ate at all, even her garlic. It seemed as though she was trying to punish herself for letting that terrible thing happen to Abu.

Zenny and I both began to feel like we'd sunk to the bottom of a well and couldn't climb out. I guess we were beginning to give up too, just like Auntie Hata. Zenny stopped watering the cucumbers, and I stopped picking them.

"Let them rot," we both said. And they did.

One evening when I was washing the supper dishes, the old man came to the back door with two of his kites. One was the diamond kite with the cross-eyed samurai who looked as if he'd just swallowed some of Dr. Oniki's awful brown medicine for stomach flu. The other was the yellow-and-black butterfly I'd seen hanging from the rafters of the barn.

"Anybody interested in flying these before it gets dark?" he asked.

"Yeah, me!" Zenny yelled, and I saw the life suddenly come back to his face.

I noticed right away that the old man had only two kites. He's leaving me out again, I thought. But the old man thrust the butterfly kite toward me and said, "Well, come on, Rinko. Hurry up and dry your hands. I'll help you get this one up."

"Me?"

"Yes, you!"

I shook the suds from my hands, wiped them on my skirt, and ran out into the fields with Zenny and the old man. The sun had bleached the weeds so they seemed almost white, and the breeze was making them rustle, as if they were whispering to each other. Auntie Hata probably would have said that was exactly what they were doing.

The old man held the samurai kite high over his head, angling it to catch the breeze, while Zenny held the spool with the flying line and backed away from him.

"Now," the old man shouted, and Zenny gave the kite a sharp tug. The samurai kite darted around for a while as if it weren't sure which way to go, and then it began to climb.

I could hardly wait to get my hands on the butterfly kite, but I watched as the old man stood with his back to the breeze and tossed it into the air. The wind lifted it right up as though it belonged in the sky, and pretty soon the butterfly was climbing.

Finally the old man handed me the spool. "Hold the line taut," he said, "and if the butterfly asks for more, feed it to her a little at a time. Understand?"

"Yes, OK," I said, turning to him.

But the old man was watching the kite. "Keep your eyes on the kite, Rinko," he said. "Listen to what it tells you."

Pretty soon I could feel the butterfly tugging at my line like a living thing, telling me it wanted to climb. So I fed out the line little by little and my butterfly soared higher and higher, it's tail dancing, until it was a small black speck in the sky.

All of a sudden I understood what the old man meant

that day he was making his samurai kite. I really felt as though I was the butterfly up there and it was *me* flying in the sky. I felt like I was part of the sky and part of the entire universe and I guessed that included the spirit world as well.

I was so busy getting my thoughts together in my head, I didn't even hear the old man telling me it was time to bring down our kites. Or rather, I guess I heard him, but I didn't want to listen because I didn't want the magical feeling to end. I wanted it to go on forever.

When I finally wound in my kite, the old man gave me a pat on the head and told me I had flown the butterfly well.

"We'll do it again someday," he said.

And I knew at last I had become his friend and that now maybe he would trust me.

I felt so good then, I thought everything was going to work out. But that was because I didn't know that a fourth bad thing was just about to happen.

11

THE NEXT MORNING, BEFORE AUNTIE
Hata left for the hospital, I heard a car drive up out in
front. I looked out the window to see if maybe Mama
and Papa had closed the laundry and repair shop and
come out to see us. But it wasn't Papa's Model T out in
front. It was a small blue coupe. And a tall blonde lady
dressed in a navy blue suit came out of it. She was
wearing a hat with a red feather, and she was carrying a
briefcase.

The minute I saw her I felt as if somebody had
grabbed my heart and given it a hard squeeze. In fact I
got the same tight feeling in my stomach and throat that
I get when I'm sick and I see Dr. Oniki walk into my
room.

I think anybody carrying a briefcase or a small black
bag is usually bad news. Except, of course, the Watkins
man. His black bag is filled with nice things like vanilla
and lemon extract and spices and chocolate bars. Some-

89

times, if Mama has extra kitchen money, she'll buy a
bottle of vanilla extract from him and then her sponge
cakes really taste good. It's one of Mama's little extrav-
agances that she doesn't mention to Papa. But I happen
to know about it.

Well, anyhow, when I saw that blonde lady coming
up the walk, I had a feeling she had nothing but trouble
inside her briefcase. Good grief, I thought, I hope she's
not another bad thing. "It's only supposed to be three,"
I said, as though Mama were standing right there next
to me.

As things turned out, I was right. The blonde lady
turned out to be nothing but bad news.

"My name is Mrs. Saunders," she said. "I'm from
the county welfare office. The hospital sent me. Is your
mother home?"

I started to tell her my mother was in Berkeley probably doing a big wash in the basement, and that I was
only visiting temporarily to help Auntie Hata over a bad
time. But Mrs. Saunders gave me a cold chill and I didn't
feel like enlightening her.

Her eyes didn't smile when her mouth did, and everything on her face looked pinched and pointed—her nose,
her thin lips, even her earlobes. I knew Auntie Hata
wouldn't like her earlobes.

"Just a minute," I said, pretending to be Auntie
Hata's daughter. "I'll go get her."

Auntie Hata was in a hurry to get to the hospital, but
she was polite enough to ask Mrs. Saunders to sit down.

90

"Will you go fix some tea, Rinko?" she asked.

"Now? In the morning?" I'd never made tea for company this early in the day.

But Auntie Hata said the kettle was still hot, so I made some tea, put it on a tray, and hurried back to the living room so I wouldn't miss anything.

Mrs. Saunders had her briefcase open and was writing a lot of things on a long form. I knew she'd already talked to our minister because she said, "Reverend Mitaka tells me you lost your husband recently. I'm sorry."

She asked Auntie Hata a lot of questions, like what her monthly income was. So Auntie Hata got the notebook she keeps in the kitchen drawer and showed her how much the factory paid her last month.

"How will you manage now that you've lost your truck?" Mrs. Saunders asked next. "And what will you do in the winter when there are no more cucumbers?"

She seemed to know almost everything about Auntie Hata, but still she kept asking questions as though she was trying to turn Auntie Hata inside out and see everything. She wanted to know how much rent Auntie Hata paid for the house, and how she could possibly afford to feed and clothe three children.

"Not three children. Only two," Auntie Hata tried to explain.

She was having trouble with her English and it was too complicated for her to explain who I was. So I finally had to tell who I was and why I was there.

"I see," Mrs. Saunders said, looking me up and down as though she was inspecting a piece of meat.

Then she stood up and asked if she could look around. And without waiting for Auntie Hata to say yes, she began walking through the house. Her high heels clicked on the floor and I saw her jot something else on her form, probably, "no carpets."

When she finished inspecting the second floor, she said, "I see you have no bathing facilities."

"Yes, we do," I said immediately, because she said it as though she thought we didn't keep ourselves clean.

I told her about the tin tub and how we could take a bath outdoors and listen to the crickets and see the stars.

"Sometimes," I added, "you can even see the spirit lights flickering out in the fields." I threw that in even if I had seen no such thing, because I thought it might shake her up a bit.

But she just said, "Well, that might do in the summer, but it's hardly adequate." And she wrote down something else, probably, "no bathtub!"

By now I could see that Auntie Hata was getting upset with this woman and anxious to go see Abu. So I gathered up my courage and became the strong, brave person I like to be.

"Auntie Hata has to go see Abu at the hospital now," I said. "And she has to walk a mile to the streetcar stop, and maybe wait a half hour for the streetcar to come."

I looked at Mrs. Saunders' face and then out at her car. I hoped she'd get the hint.

Her eyebrows wiggled up like two thin worms, and she said, "Well, I could take her to the streetcar stop."

"Or even to the hospital would be nice," I said, surprising myself.

"Well, we'll see," she said.

I saw she wasn't promising anything, but I pushed Auntie Hata toward the door so they could get going before Mrs. Saunders changed her mind.

Auntie Hata bowed and thanked her, and the two of them went riding off in the blue coupe. But I had a feeling we hadn't seen the last of Mrs. Saunders. She was probably going to stir up a lot more trouble, I thought, and make Auntie Hata feel worse.

I got so upset thinking about that, I decided to write Tami about it. I'd begun a letter to her the day after I arrived and added a little each day. I was on page fifteen now and still hadn't finished. Each time I thought I was ready to mail the letter, something else happened and I had to write about that.

I'd already written about Abu's accident and about the old man and how he'd finally let me fly one of his kites and be his friend. Now I had to tell her about the welfare lady who turned out to be the fourth bad thing.

What a pain in the neck Mrs. Sourpuss was! She didn't have one nice thing to say about Auntie Hata's house, and it's not that bad. In fact, I'm getting to like this funny creaky old house—probably inhabited by many spirits. [I knew this last would really

93

make Tami curious.] *And I'm getting to like Auntie Hata. She is not crazy, the way you always say. She is just eccentric.* [Like your mama, I almost wrote but didn't.]

I know Auntie Hata doesn't want to go on welfare. Who would? I want to think of a way to help her. I'm thinking maybe I should ask Mama to pray for some kind of miracle.

'I'm also thinking I'd better end this letter and mail it, or I'll get back to Berkeley before it does.

Write back immediately. There is a mailbox out here!

> *Your loving friend.*
> *Rinko Evangeline Tsujimura*

P.S. How do you like my new middle name? I really wanted to be Rinko Anne, but I didn't want to go through life being a R.A.T.

12

•-•--•-•--•-•--•-•--•-•--•-•--•-•--•-•--•-•--•-•--•-•--•-•--•-•--•-•--•-•--•-•--•-•--•-•--•-•

AUNTIE HATA WAITED UNTIL SUPPER-
time to make her announcement, just the way Mama
does.

"I guess we'll have to do it," she said.

She didn't even bother to put garlic on her rice and
was poking at the fried mackerel on her plate, pulling
out the tiny bones one by one with her chopsticks the way
I was doing.

"Do what, Ma?" Zenny asked.

His fish-eating technique was different. He took a big
mouthful and then had to spit out the bones. That's why
I'm not crazy about eating fish. You either have to work
hard picking out the bones before you can even eat a
mouthful or end up looking as if you swallowed a pin-
cushion—like Zenny. Maybe I'm just lazy, but I don't
like eating things with a lot of little seeds either, like
grapes and watermelons. That's because I'm not like my
brother Joji, who just swallows all the seeds and will
probably sprout grapes in his stomach one of these days.

95

"I don't want to, you know," Auntie Hata went on. She sounded beaten down and weary. "But what can I do?"

I tried asking this time. "Do what, Auntie Hata?"

"Go on welfare." She seemed to shrivel up and shrink when she said that. "Mrs. Saunders says she'll find us a small house downtown—one with a bathtub. And she's going to help me find work, maybe in one of the laundries on Eighth Street."

Zenny stopped eating. "Well, I ain't moving!" He scowled. "Who wants a bathtub, anyway? And besides, what'll the old man do if we leave "

Auntie Hata looked like a bird whose nest had been discovered. "Did you tell the welfare lady about the old man?" she asked me.

"No. Why?"

"He doesn't like people poking around in his affairs."

"Why not?"

"He has his reasons."

Auntie Hata clammed up then and wouldn't say another word. And that was when I decided I was going to find out for myself that very minute.

"I'm going to ask the old man right now," I said. And I left my bony mackerel sitting half eaten on my plate and ran out the back door.

"Rinko, come back!" I heard Auntie Hata calling to me.

But I kept right on going. I pulled open the barn door and yelled, "It's me, Rinko. Are you home?"

The old man was fixing himself a cup of tea. "Ah, good evening, Rinko," he said. "How is Abu today?"

I could see we were going to have a little polite conversation before I could blurt out my question. So I told him Abu was better but still couldn't use his right hand.

"Will you have a cup of tea with me?" he asked then.

"Sure."

I was hoping he would produce something like a cookie or a sweet bean paste cake to go with it, but all he did was get out his long, thin Japanese pipe. It held just a thimbleful of tobacco, and he tamped it in and puffed slowly. We both watched the long curl of white smoke drift up to the rafters.

"It looks like a ghost," I said.

"Probably come to visit us from the spirit world," the old man answered.

"You believe in spirits then?" I asked. "I mean, do you think they come back from the land of the dead to visit us?"

"Of course. Didn't I tell you we are all one in this universe? That means the living and the spirits of the dead as well."

"Oh."

Silence.

"Old man, are you ever afraid?"

"Of the spirits?"

"Of anything. . . ."

"Only of things I cannot control myself."

Ask him now, I said to myself. Ask him now what he

97

is so afraid of that he can't tell. I took a deep breath, opened my mouth, and that is when Zenny came bursting into the barn.

"Old man! Old man! Mama says the welfare lady is going to make us move downtown!" he yelled.

The old man got the same startled look that had crossed Auntie Hata's face. "What welfare lady? When did she come?" And he asked us dozens of questions until we'd told him everything about Mrs. Saunders and her visit.

The old man suddenly got up and began pacing up and down. "Welfare!" He spat out the word like a worm from a rotten apple. "They will rob you of your soul and dignity. Did you tell the woman about me? Did you tell her I lived in the barn?"

"No, no. We didn't say anything," I said.

But the old man's face was scrunched up with worry. So finally I asked, "What is it you're so afraid of anyway, old man?"

"Yeah, what?" Zenny echoed, the way Abu does.

The old man sat down, thought a few minutes, and said he'd tell us if we promised solemnly never to tell another living soul.

"May God strike me dead if I ever tell," I said and felt a shiver go down my back as I said that.

"Same here," Zenny said. "Scout's honor, cross my heart, and hope to die."

We both held up our right hands, as though we were swearing to tell the truth and nothing but the truth to a judge.

"Well then," the old man said. And he began as though he were telling us a story.

"When I was only seventeen, I ran away from home because I didn't want to spend the rest of my days working in the rice paddies like my father," he began. "I went to the big port city of Yokohama and found a job on a freighter as a cook."

He looked at us with a half smile. "You understand I had never so much as cooked a pot of rice before, but once the ship sailed they were stuck with me, and I learned fast."

"Well, I sailed around the world twice, and one day when my freighter docked in San Francisco, I jumped ship and never went back. I didn't know anything then. I didn't know about getting immigration papers. All I knew was that I wanted to earn some money in the 'golden land.' "

"And go back to Japan a rich man?" I asked. I'd heard that part from some of Papa's friends who'd hoped for the same thing.

"Something like that." The old man nodded.

Then he told how he couldn't find a job in San Francisco and signed up with a work crew going to the copper mines in Utah.

"*Yah*, what a job that was," he groaned. "I thought my back would break, and I was actually glad when the foreman fired me."

"So you came back to California?" I asked, hurrying him along. I wanted him to get to the bad part—to the thing that was making him afraid.

99

"That's when you picked onions and sugar beets and grapes in the valley," Zenny interrupted. I guess he'd heard that part before.

"I breathed dust every day and was scorched by the sun for ten years before I gave up and came to Oakland," the old man explained.

"And then you came to The Eagle Cafe?"

"After I'd washed a lot of dishes and swept a lot of dirty floors."

I couldn't wait any longer. "So then, what are you afraid of, old man?"

He finally leaned toward Zenny and me, and his voice sounded like two pieces of sandpaper being rubbed together.

"You see, I never did get my papers because I learned there was a quota for Japanese immigrants. I learned America didn't want us, and I thought I'd get deported if I made my presence known."

The old man stopped and looked hard at Zenny and me.

"So you see, I have been an illegal alien all these years. And I still am."

Illegal! It was like hearing a fingernail scratched across a blackboard just to hear that word. "You mean they could send you to jail if they catch you?"

"Perhaps. Or send me back to Japan in disgrace. You see now why I can't have well-meaning ministers or welfare workers snooping around and asking me questions."

100

I felt as if a light bulb had just flashed over my head the way it does over people in the comic strips, and I understood everything. No wonder the old man kept his distance from strangers. No wonder it took so long for him to trust me as a friend.

"I'll never tell," Zenny swore.

"Me neither," I said.

I clapped my hand over my mouth, looking like one of the three monkeys who don't see, hear, or speak evil. But all the time I was swearing not to tell, I could feel his secret jumping around inside me dying to get out. If only I could just tell Papa, I thought. I knew he'd find a way to help the old man.

I knew Papa would understand his dream of wanting to go back to Japan a rich man. And I was sure the old man would like Papa. They both had the same force in the core of their beings that made them brave and strong. Also Papa wasn't crazy about ministers either. They had a lot in common.

But it was as though the old man could see inside my skull, just like Mama, and knew what I was thinking. "You are to tell no one," he said. "Do not betray me. Only the two of you and Zenny's mama know about me now."

And then he became cold and aloof again, as though he was sorry he'd trusted us with his secret after all. He pushed back his chair and said almost to himself, "Well, perhaps it is time. . . ."

"For what?"

101

But the old man made it clear the conversation had come to an end, and Zenny and I knew it was time to go.

My whole body felt heavy when I walked out of the barn, as though it was weighted down now by the old man's secret. It was as if a big heavy stone occupied the pit of my stomach where the core of my energy was supposed to be. And now I felt the same fear the old man had lived with for so many years.

13

AUNTIE HATA DIDN'T SAY ANYTHING
more about Mrs. Saunders or going on welfare or moving. Whenever Zenny asked about it, she'd just say,
"We'll work something out. Don't worry." And she'd
talk about Abu instead. "He's eating more now," she'd
say. Or, "The color is coming back to his face."

Then one night I woke up out of a sound sleep. I was
dreaming that a strange white light had drifted in
through the window from the fields and was blowing its
cold, icy breath all over me. I was sure it was one of
Zenny's spirits come to get me and was about to scream
when I woke up. I discovered I'd kicked off all my
covers and was shivering with cold.

I jumped out of bed and closed the window. I also took
a good look out in the fields, but they were pitch dark
and I didn't see even a tiny flicker.

It was when I climbed back into bed that I heard footsteps downstairs. Maybe it was one of those hobos who

103

come around asking for food, I thought. Auntie Hata usually shooed them off saying, "No food. No food." But maybe one of them had sneaked inside the house.

Then I thought I heard Auntie Hata's voice. Was she down there talking to a hobo, I wondered. What if he had a knife and was demanding some money? My heart started to pound and my mouth felt as dry as a summer vineyard.

Sometimes when I'm scared, I try to imagine how my big brother would act in the same situation. Then I try to behave the way he would. That night I imagined what the old man might do. He'd march right downstairs and heave the hobo out of the house, probably. I knew I couldn't do that, but at least I could go down and see if Auntie Hata needed help.

I wished I had Joji's baseball bat to take with me but found a coat hanger in the closet instead. It wasn't much of a weapon, but I clutched it and started tiptoeing down the stairs. Every time I took a step the stair would creak and groan, as though the old house were talking to me and telling me to be careful. I held my breath and listened so hard my ears ached.

Then I heard Auntie Hata's voice as clear as a bell. "So what do you think, Papa?"

When I heard that, I almost died right there on the steps. I knew Mr. Hata wasn't sitting in the urn on the mantel. I knew he was buried in the cemetery. So then it had to be his spirit, probably sitting on the sofa in a ghostly white light.

104

I don't know how I got down the rest of those stairs, because I certainly don't remember walking. But suddenly, there I was in the parlor with a coat hanger clutched in my hand.

And there was Auntie Hata standing in her white night kimono and slippers, her long hair hanging down her back. She looked like a ghostly spirit herself. She was standing in front of Mr. Hata's photo on the mantel with her hands clasped together as though she was praying. But she wasn't talking to God, of course. She was talking to Mr. Hata as though he was right there and as much a part of her life as he'd ever been.

"What shall I do, Papa?" she asked. "I really don't want to go on welfare. I want to take care of our family myself. And someday I want to go see our Teru in Japan and bring her back with me. I need to earn money to do that. Oh, Papa, what shall I do?"

That's when I heard myself pipe up, "Then don't go on welfare, Auntie Hata. Mama and Papa will help you find a job."

I didn't have the faintest notion how they could do that, but the words just came out of my mouth as if somebody had put them there. And I nearly scared the wits out of Auntie Hata.

"*Mah*, Rinko, you scared me half to death," she gasped. And she had to sit down and pat her chest to calm down her heart.

"I'm sorry, Auntie Hata," I said. "The words just popped out. As though maybe Mr. Hata put them there."

105

"Really? You know his spirit *did* seem very close just now."

"Well, maybe he did then," I said. And then another light bulb flashed over my head. "Maybe I am his medium," I said. "You know, like a go-between."

A chill shriveled my scalp and went down my backbone when I said that. Suppose I really was a medium and could communicate with the dead? I immediately thought of all the people in the spirit world I would like to contact, like maybe my samurai great-grandfather, or maybe Abraham Lincoln. Maybe I could get a crystal ball, drape a scarf around my head, and hold seances in our parlor. Maybe. . . .

I suddenly realized Auntie Hata was talking to me the way she would to Mama or Papa.

"Rinko, do you think I could ever find the kind of work your mama used to do? You know, working for a white family?"

"Sure. Why not?"

"But my English isn't good like your mama's, and I can only cook Japanese foods like rice and *miso* soup. How could I work for a white family?"

"Mama could show you how to cook American stuff."

"But I need money right now. Next week. How am I going to manage?"

I was trying hard to think how. I thought I was sitting there listening to Auntie Hata and concentrating on her problem. But the next thing I knew, she was shaking me and telling me to go back to bed, which I did. And the next morning I wondered if I had dreamed the whole thing, because Auntie Hata didn't say anything more about our midnight conversation.

When Auntie Hata came home from the hospital the next day, she looked happier than I'd seen her look in a long time.

"Abu's coming home Sunday," she said. "Your mama and papa are picking us up at the hospital."

She told Zenny to go tell the old man, but it was Zenny's turn to wash the dishes, and he was still scrubbing the rice pot. So I offered to go tell the old man.

I ran to the barn, swung open the door, and yelled, "Hey, old man, guess what! Abu's coming home Sunday!"

I knew he should have been home by now, but the old man didn't answer.

"Old man?" I called again.

I walked to the back of the barn and looked at his table and cot. Everything was clean and neat, as though he'd just cleaned house and put everything away. There were no teacups or dishes on the table, and there weren't any pots of paint or paste either.

Everything was too quiet and too neat, and I had the strange feeling something was wrong. I looked up and saw all the bright kites still hanging there, but everything else in the barn seemed different.

I was just about to leave when I noticed the envelope on the old man's pillow. It was a letter for Auntie Hata. I grabbed it and raced back to the house, yelling, "The old man's gone! He's left you a letter!"

"What?" Auntie Hata said. "Here, let me see."

107

She couldn't afford eyeglasses, so she had to hold the letter way out and squint at the Japanese writing. She was reading it to herself until Zenny said, "Out loud, Ma. Read it out loud."

"My good friends, Mrs. Hata, Zenichiro, Abraham, and Rinko," she began.

"I have decided the time has come for me to go home and to stop living in fear. I realize now that it is not necessary to return to Japan a rich man. It is more important to return home with my dignity and pride intact. So I am leaving as I came, by freighter.

"I do not like good-byes, so I have taken my bag with me this morning, and I shall not return this night.

"Mrs. Hata, be strong, and do not let the welfare people rob you of your pride and soul. I leave before they come to claim mine."

Auntie Hata sighed. "Ah, old man, we shall miss you."

"I never told," I wailed. "Mrs. Saunders never knew. Papa could have helped him."

"Won't he ever come back?" Zenny wondered.

Auntie Hata shook her head. "Probably not, Zenny. But listen, he left something for you and Abu." And she finished reading the letter.

"I am leaving all my kites for you boys. But the butterfly is for Rinko. Fly them well and think of me. Stay well. Stay free. Your friend, Mankichi Yamanaka."

"Why'd he have to go, anyway?" I asked. I was mad at him now. We hadn't told his secret. Not to anybody.

"It's all that dumb welfare lady's fault," Zenny said, kicking at a chair leg. "She never shoulda come here."

108

And he ran out to make sure the old man was really gone. I could hear him calling to the old man all the way to the barn.

I felt as though the old man had deserted me just when I'd finally become his friend. I guess Auntie Hata knew I was feeling empty inside, as if somebody had scooped everything out.

"Don't fret, Rinko," she said quietly. "There is a time for everything, you know, and it was time for the old man to go home where he belongs."

She was quiet for a minute, as if she was feeling a lot of things herself. Then she said, "You have to learn to let go of people sometimes, even if you're not ready to."

The way she'd had to let go of Mr. Hata, I thought. But what I said was, "He could at least have come to say good-bye."

Auntie Hata shook her head. "That's not his way, Rinko. Besides, he left his butterfly for you, didn't he? You've got his butterfly to remember him by, haven't you?"

"Uh-huh."

"Well, then. . . ."

"You know something, Auntie Hata," I said. "This is the fifth bad thing that's happened since I came here. My ankle, Abu's arm, the truck, Mrs. Saunders, and now the old man."

I was expecting Auntie Hata to say that meant we had one more bad thing coming to complete the cycle. But she surprised me again.

She just said, "You know, Rinko, sometimes what you

think is a bad thing isn't bad at all. It turns out to be a good thing."

"Name one," I said.

She didn't take long. "All right," she said. "The old man's leaving may seem like a bad thing for you. But it's not for him. It's a fine thing that he can go home and not be afraid anymore, don't you think?"

"I guess so."

"Then be happy for him."

I couldn't just yet, so I ran out to the barn and found Zenny looking up at all the kites. The butterfly wasn't hanging on the rafters where I'd seen it before. It was hanging right over the old man's cot, as though he'd moved it there especially for me.

"There's yours," Zenny said, pointing.

"I know."

I lifted it down carefully and carried it back to my room. I looked at it for a long time, remembering the time the old man and I flew it together in the fields, and finally I stopped feeling mad at him. I guessed maybe he knew all along that I hate saying good-bye too.

14

THE MORNING AFTER THE OLD MAN
left, Mrs. Saunders came back, and I knew Auntie Hata
was right. It *was* a good thing the old man left when he
did. Maybe Mrs. Saunders might have marched into
the barn and started asking questions that very day and
the old man might have ended up in her clutches.

"I came with the forms," Mrs. Saunders said, getting
right down to business.

I went to the kitchen to get some tea before Auntie
Hata had to ask me. There was nothing to serve with it,
and I thought how good one of Mrs. Sugar's spice cookies
would taste that very minute. But of course there weren't
any.

I opened all the cupboards to see if there was anything
interesting around. But no such luck. All I found was a
jar full of garlic. I was tempted to bring out a plateful
of garlic with the tea, just to see the look on Mrs. Saunders' face. But she'd probably write "no food in the
house" on her form, so I decided not to.

Zenny was heading for the front door when I brought in the tea. "I'll go look for some firewood, Ma," he said. And I knew he was trying to escape.

But his mother told him to sit down. "You too, Rinko," she said. She was taking charge again, like that time at the hospital.

So the four of us sat in the parlor as though we were having a tea party. Mrs. Saunders took a blue fountain pen from her purse and handed it to Auntie Hata.

"There," she said, pointing to a line at the bottom of her form. "You sign right there. If you can't sign your name, an X will do."

Auntie Hata straightened up in her chair and smoothed out the wrinkles in her dress. "I know how to sign my name," she said. "But I not do."

I could see Auntie Hata's English wasn't coming out today.

"But, Mrs. Hata, you don't seem to understand," Mrs. Saunders said. "Everything is arranged. I've found a house for you downtown. We will take care of you. Sign here."

Auntie Hata shook her head. "My husband tell me I can take care of family myself. I no sign. Thank you."

Mrs. Saunders looked as though she'd been shoved into a swimming pool with all her clothes on. Her mouth was open, but no words came out. Finally she sputtered, "Your husband? I thought he was dead. What I mean to say is. . . ." And then she thought she knew what had happened. "Oh, I see. You've remarried then. You have someone to take care of you now."

We just sat there and let Mrs. Saunders talk on and on until she thought she had everything all figured out. She stuffed her papers back into her briefcase and didn't even bother to drink her tea.

"You should have told me you had some means of support now," she said in a huff. "I spent a great deal of time working on your case."

She was talking so fast, I knew Auntie Hata didn't understand a word she was saying. Auntie Hata just sat there, smiling and nodding, and finally she stood up and said, "Thank you very much," to let Mrs. Saunders know there was nothing more to say.

We all trooped out to the front porch and watched Mrs. Saunders drive off in her blue coupe.

"Good riddance!" Zenny shouted.

"To bad rubbish!" I finished.

And then we both let out a huge whoop.

"We really ain't goin' on welfare then, Ma?" Zenny asked.

"Your papa said not to," I explained. "He told me to tell your mama not to."

"Aw, that's a lot of baloney." I could tell Zenny wasn't sure, in spite of what he'd told me about seeing the spirit lights.

"Maybe not so much baloney as you think, Zenny," Auntie Hata said on my behalf. But before I could get too bigheaded about my wonderful accomplishment, Auntie Hata said, "Let's go have some more rice and soup. Saving my soul from the welfare lady has suddenly given me an appetite."

113

And she headed straight for the kitchen cupboard, got out some garlic, and chopped it up. I knew then that Auntie Hata was going to be OK. And I thought the old man would have been proud of her for not losing her soul to the welfare lady. Now all we had to do was find Auntie Hata a job.

I believe good things usually happen on Sundays. And I discovered that they happen even if you don't go to church every Sunday. This was a great revelation to me, because I always thought God made good things happen only if a person went to church without fail. Only if you went even in the pouring rain or froze in that icebox of a church with the puny furnace that wouldn't even heat a closet. I always thought good things happened like a sort of reward.

I hadn't gone to Sunday School once during the entire month I was at Auntie Hata's. I thought maybe that was why all those bad things kept happening.

But finally the good things began to come. Auntie Hata had gotten rid of the welfare lady, and Abu was coming home. I hoped maybe good things happened in threes too and that we'd have one more.

Auntie Hata went to the hospital early, and Mama and Papa and Joji were going there right after church to bring her home with Abu. I was counting on Mama to bring a picnic basket full of chicken and rice balls, and maybe even a sponge cake for dessert.

My month was up and school would be starting soon, so I was going home with Mama and Papa that afternoon.

I could hardly wait to ask Mama and Papa if they couldn't produce a miracle and help Auntie Hata find a job. But I sort of dreaded seeing Abu.

Ever since I'd seen him at the hospital, looking so pale and weak, I had this awful feeling he'd never be the same again. I know how terrible I'd feel if I couldn't ever use my right hand anymore. I wouldn't be able to write in my diary or write letters or fly a kite or help Mama with the washing and ironing. I'd probably want to climb in a dark hole, pull a lid over it, and never come out again, ever. I wondered if Abu would still laugh and talk the way he used to.

I guess Zenny was worried too, because he spent the whole morning chopping firewood without his mama having to tell him to.

What I did was to iron some clean sheets and pillowcases and put them on Abu's bed as a sort of welcome home.

The minute we heard Papa's Model T come rattling down the road, Zenny and I went running out to meet it.

"Hey, Abu! Joji! Mama! Papa!" I was yelling, and Zenny was yelling, and both of us were jumping around and acting kind of crazy because we didn't quite know what to do.

I could see Abu sitting in the back seat between Mama and Auntie Hata all wrapped up in a blanket.

Joji was the first one out of the car, and the minute he opened the back door, Abu threw off his blanket and pushed his way past his mama to get out. His right arm was still in a sling, and he looked as if he hadn't seen the sun in a long time. But there was a big grin on his face and he was wearing new glasses. I guess somebody at the hospital got them for him.

"Hey, I'm home! I'm home!" he yelled.

Everybody piled out of the car then, and there was so much shouting and hugging and crying all around that for a minute I forgot I hadn't seen Joji in almost a month.

"Hey, Joj," I said poking him in the ribs. "You been messing around in my room?"

He poked me back. "Sure have, Rinky-dink. Read all the old diaries you got stashed away in your closet."

"You what?" I was ready to skin him alive. "You know those diaries are my personal and private property, Joji. You had no right—"

"April fool! Got ya, din't I?"

He certainly had, and he thought it was hilarious. So I simply gave him the most disgusted look I could manage and turned to ask Mama if she'd brought some lunch.

"Of course," Mama said, like I knew she would. "And there's sponge cake for dessert."

I waited until after we'd finished Mama's rice balls and gingered chicken, and we'd put Abu to bed for a nap between his nice, smooth sheets. Then I planned to tell Mama and Papa all about Mrs. Saunders and how Auntie Hata had sent her packing and needed a job immediately.

But Papa beat me to it. He knew all about everything. I guess Mrs. Saunders had talked to Reverend Mitaka,

116

and he told Papa everything. The best part came next. Mama and Papa actually did produce a miracle.

"The Japanese bachelors in our church dormitory need someone to cook and clean house for them," Papa said to Auntie Hata. "They want to chip in and pay your salary."

"Did you say *my* salary?" Auntie Hata asked, surprised.

"Yes." Mama nodded. "The job is yours if you want it."

"I wouldn't have to know English to work there, would I? And I could cook Japanese food for them, couldn't I?"

"That's exactly what they're longing for," Mama said.

"Then we wouldn't have to move?" Zenny asked.

"Not if your mama is willing to take the streetcar to the dormitory every day."

"Oh, I'm willing. I'm willing." Auntie Hata beamed.

Papa beamed back at her. "Good. Then it's all settled."

And there it was. Good thing number three had happened, just like that. Auntie Hata's problems were solved.

I went up to say good-bye to Abu before we left. He was half asleep but he asked, "Y'want my turtle, Herbert?"

I really didn't want a turtle, but I knew it was a big thing for Abu to offer it to me. So I got Abu's turtle from his box on the windowsill and stuck him in my

117

pocket, where he wiggled around a bit before settling down.

"Thanks, Abu," I said. "I think I'll change his name to Abraham in your honor."

Abu grinned. "OK," he said. "And I'll get me another turtle and call it Rinky-dink."

"Shake," I said.

Abu stuck out his left hand. "Shake, yourself," he said. This time he had a good strong grip, and I knew he was going to be OK.

When it was time to go, Auntie Hata thanked me for all the help I'd been.

"It was wonderful having a daughter, even for one month," she said. And she gave me a hug that smelled like strawberries. I guess the pomade was on her hair that day and not on her shoes.

"I'll come again anytime you need me, until your real daughter Teru comes back," I promised. And I meant it.

Papa helped me carry all my stuff down to the car. But I carried the butterfly kite myself, holding it high so the tail wouldn't drag.

"Hey, bring that the next time ya come and we'll go fly kites," Zenny said.

I guessed it was sort of an invitation, so I promised I would.

When Mama and Auntie Hata were finished with the bowing and leave-taking talk, we all piled in the car, Papa cranked up the motor, and we started down the road.

118

I leaned out of the car waving and yelling, "So long, Auntie Hata! So long, Zenny! So long, Abu!" And something made me holler, "So long, Mr. Hata!"

Joji turned around and gave me one of his looks. "You musta caught being crazy from Mrs. Hata." He smirked.

"Since you're so smart, Joji Tsujimura, I'll tell you something," I shot back. "Mrs. Hata is not the least bit crazy. In fact she's a brave lady, and she's got a lot more sense than you'll ever have."

I saw Mama smiling to herself. And Papa said, "Well, I'm glad you learned that while you were out here, Rinko."

"I learned something else too," I said. "I learned that I am a medium and can communicate with the dead."

Of course nobody in the Model T Ford believed that for one minute—not Mama or Papa or Joji.

"Aw, baloney!" Joji muttered.

But I knew it wasn't all baloney. I truly believe Mr. Hata's spirit *was* there that night and that he truly did speak to Auntie Hata through me.

I could hardly wait to tell Cal when he got home, and Mrs. Sugar, to see what she'd make of the whole thing. But mostly, I could hardly wait to see the look on my friend Tami's face when I told her about my new talent, which I knew was something she didn't have.

I felt so wise and brilliant then, I decided I would enlighten everybody about one more thing. "You know something else? Good things also happen in threes."

119

"Oh?" Mama said.

"One, Abu's home and he's OK. Two, Auntie Hata's not on welfare and she's got a job. Three, the old man's going home and never has to be afraid anymore."

"What old man?" Joji asked immediately.

I almost blurted out his whole story, including his secret, then and there. But I could almost hear the old man telling me not to tell another living soul. And I felt as though if I told now, he'd lose his dignity after all. And maybe I'd lose mine too for betraying him. So I kept my mouth shut.

"He's a good friend," I explained. "And he gave me a kite to remember him by."

Before Joji could pester me with more questions about the old man, I quickly said, "And another thing. Bad things aren't always bad. Sometimes they turn out to be good."

"Of course," Mama said. "That's often true."

"More often than not," Papa added.

"Like what?" Joji wanted to know.

"Like going to Auntie Hata's," I said, remembering how Mama'd had to coax me to go. "It was the best bad thing that ever happened to me."

And that is an absolutely true fact.

120